HAVE YOURSELF A MERRY LITTLE WITNESS

MARSHMALLOW HOLLOW MYSTERIES BOOK 2

DAKOTA CASSIDY

COPYRIGHT

Welcome to Marshmallow Hollow Mysteries! Set in the wintery, seaside (and totally fictional) town of Marshmallow Hollow, Maine, where it's all Christmas all the time, and murder is hung by the chimney with care! I'm so excited to introduce you to Halliday Valentine (Hal for short), Atticus Finch—her crusty hummingbird familiar—her small gang of crime solvers, and the quirky folks from her beloved hometown.

Please note, this series is a bit of a spinoff of my *Witchless in Seattle* series, in that Hal and part of the gang were introduced in book 10 of the series, titled *Witch It Real Good*. But there's no need to read the *Witchless* series if you haven't.

That said, this is an ongoing series (not a stand-alone) and there will be some underlying mysteries that will linger from book to book, but I promise to wrap up the central mystery with a big, fat bow by each book's end! Also note, I'm taking artistic license with places and names of things in the beautiful state of Maine—thus, any and all mistakes are mine and certainly not meant to offend.

Lastly, Christmas is my absolute favorite time of the year. I love everything about it, from the decorations, the music, the gathering of friends and family, and most of all, the hope the season brings.

I hope you all love Hal, her friends, and her tiny little Christmas town as much as I do!

Dakota XXOO

ACKNOWLEDGEMENTS

Cover artist: Katie Wood
Editor: Kelli Collins

CHAPTER 1

The Christmas Song
    Written by Mel Tormé and Robert Wells during a
blistering-hot summer in 1945

"There's a light out on the strand of bulbs above the kitchen cabinets, Halliday. Do handle it, would you, please? It throws the entire balance of the greenery and ornaments off and looks positively dreadful," said Atticus, of the deep voice and even deeper disapproval, as we finished up the last of our Christmas decorating.

I rolled my eyes at my hummingbird, who hovered in my sightline, his wings buzzing. "Yes, Drama Queen. I'll get to it as soon as I'm sure these pictures are straight."

Taking a step back from the batch of vintage Santa

pictures I'd just hung along each side of the fireplace, I sighed with disgust. "I have zero sense of symmetry."

"Not if you angle your head at four o' clock," Atticus reassured. "Maybe five after."

I cocked my head. "I don't think I can ask everyone to hold their heads at four o'clock, Atti."

"I told you to measure, Halliday."

"And I told you I never measure."

"And I told you it would be crooked."

I planted my hands on my hips and ignored him as I assessed. We were almost done with decorating the house (it only took an entire week, starting the day after Thanksgiving), and my fondest wish at this point was to be able to sit and enjoy it all. I couldn't enjoy it if the pictures were crooked.

Knowing Atti would scold me for using my magic instead of manually adjusting the frame didn't stop me from lifting my index finger in the air, moving the frame a bit to the right and straightening the picture of Santa riding a moonbeam.

"Halliday…" Atti warned.

He didn't like me to use my magic for something I could do with good old-fashioned manual labor. He was forever worried I'd forget and use it in front of someone I shouldn't, and I'd be discovered for the witch I am.

Then they'd burn me at the stake in the town square, blah, blah, blah.

I grinned at him as the picture leveled out. "What? I'm just getting my fingers warmed up for Uncle

Darling's arrival. You know he'll want to do at least one ritual altar to honor mom before he moves on to his next stop."

Uncle Darling is actually my godfather, and my mother's best friend she met while in college in Boston. His real name is Andrew Darkling, and on the drag queen circuit he's known as Tia Fortew (get it?). He's quite famous—or maybe it's infamous—in the world of hip pads and glitter.

My first real memory of Uncle Darling is of him in a blonde wig teased to the heavens, long red nails, and a beautiful sparkly red dress, with eyelashes the size of hand fans glued to his eyelids.

Apparently, his last name, Darkling, stuck, but I couldn't pronounce it properly and instead dubbed him Aunt Darling. At that age, I didn't know he was a man dressing as a woman as part of his profession.

He was simply someone I adored who showed up from time to time and played trucks and dress-up with me, and took me on long walks to the beach to gather seashells and into town for double scoops of my favorite ice cream.

Anyway, he's retired from the drag queen circuit now, but he's been a constant in my life for as far back as I can remember and I love him as much as if he were blood related.

He and my mother were as close as two best friends can be, and now that she's left the mortal realm, he's made it a point to come visit me every couple of months so we'll never lose touch.

This month, he's doing what he calls his Christmas tour—in and out in seventy-two hours or less. The one where he drops in on friends and family for a few days during the holidays (his motto is, stay any longer and, like fish, a houseguest begins to smell), lavishes them with love and gifts and whisks off to the next place, leaving behind his biting sense of humor and the memory of nonstop belly laughs over wine.

Atti grated a sigh. "You don't need your fingers for that, Halliday, and you know that quite well. Speaking of Andrew, when is he supposed to arrive?"

I looked at my phone. "In about an hour. He's driving in from New Hampshire, where they just left Monty's sister's house. So it shouldn't be long before they arrive."

Monty is Montwell Danvers, Uncle Darling's husband, who was once a lighting engineer on several of his tours. They were married four years ago in a gorgeous wedding on the beach in Bora Bora, with my mother as maid of honor and me as a bridesmaid.

Remembering it now, my portly Uncle Darling in his white shirt and crisply pleated trousers with a tall, lean Monty at his side, both of them with love brightly shining in their eyes, forced me to remember how beautiful my mother had been in her organza sea-green dress.

Backless, crisscrossed over her breasts and wrapped around her neck, the dress floated delicately in the wind as her long black hair rippled behind and her bare feet dug into the sand as the sun set and the happy couple had promised to love one another until the end of time.

Warm waves had crashed to the shore, their frothy caps slapping against the wet sand, the setting sun grazing my mother's shoulders as she silently shed happy tears because Uncle Darling, after all those years on the road, had finally found true love.

"I hope so," Atti said, interrupting my reverie. "I worry, with the weather being the way it is tonight, the pair of them will land teats up in a snowbank. It is quite dismal out, Halliday."

"You say dismal, I say picturesque."

Wandering into the kitchen to attend to the broken light above the cabinet, I looked out the windows facing the cliff my house sat on and heard the ocean crashing below. Even though the backyard was lit up at every corner with snowmen and Christmas trees, it was hazy from the snow and visibility was poor.

But did I mention Uncle Darling is a warlock? He'll clear a path if necessary because he doesn't have an Atti riding him like a bucking bronco and minding his magic at every turn.

Witchcraft could be a little sexist from time to time. Warlocks don't have familiars—it's as though the ancients thought a man could navigate this world without issue, but a helpless woman? She needed a keeper.

Not that I don't love Atti. There was never a time he wasn't around, and to say I wanted to do as I pleased without him breathing down my neck is to denounce the enrichment he brings to my life.

Without him, I'd be very sad. But I won't lie. I do mind the freedoms allowed warlocks when I'm not given the same pass.

Though, times were a-changin'. Our supreme ruler —head witch honcho, Baba Yaga—was a feminist, and while the ancients may have set the standards, she was all about blowing them up.

"Picturesque, yes. Conducive to safe driving? No, Halliday."

"It is looking pretty rough out there," I agreed, pulling the sleeves of my mid-thigh-length sweater over my cold hands with a shiver, grateful for the warmth of a crackling fire.

Atti flew up behind me with a tsk-tsk. "Though, I'll admit it's rather lovely."

Turning, I looked at my open concept kitchen/dining room in one of the biggest spaces in the house, pleased with how the decorating had gone.

With the large kitchen island behind me, I leaned back on it and smiled. I adored the long walnut stained dining room table to my left and the fireplace next to it, ten or so feet away.

I'd put two small matching buffalo-plaid armchairs in front of the glowing fire, with a small antique white table between them for the times I wanted to enjoy my morning coffee. Phil's cat tree was to the right of the fireplace so he could enjoy the warmth, but was far enough away from food preparation and well, *us*.

I plumped the pillows sitting on the chairs before I wandered over to Phil and gave my ungrateful rescue cat a stroke to his head.

As per usual, he gave me the evil eye and inched away from me.

"Is that worry I hear in your voice, Atti? Wasn't it only last week you gave me that long sigh of aggravation when I told you Uncle Darling was coming for a few days?"

"As if the day will ever come when I worry about that over-bedazzled wanderer."

I grinned. Atti, as always, had a gripe about Uncle Darling. Let's face it, Atti had a gripe about everyone, but he was especially sore with Uncle Darling for taking Mom on so many of his "pointless meanderings," as Atti called them.

But there was one meandering he had with my mother Atti would probably forever grudge about.

Uncle Darling had been a nomad for most of his life, touring as a drag queen, landing wherever the road or an airplane took him. Atti didn't like that Darling didn't have a permanent residence until he and Monty bought a place in Cape Cod five years ago.

Atticus also thinks my uncle is responsible for encouraging my mother to have an impromptu summer fling with my father. My father, Hugh Granite, is a movie star—well, in Japan. He's sort of what David Hasselhoff is to Germany, and he'll tell you so—even if you don't ask.

Anyway, my mother, Keeva, met him when he was

here in our little town, filming a movie. From what I understand, they had a whirlwind romance, but he left when the movie was done and never looked back.

She never looked back either, but she also never told him about me, or me about him. I didn't know until the reading of my mother's will and I didn't go looking for him. I was too wrapped up in my grief. However, he came looking for me.

I think it might have to do with aging and atonement, but it's not for me to judge, I suppose. I'm honest when I say, I wasn't one of those kids who wondered where her father was all the time or felt like I'd missed out on having a father. I had my grandfather and two incredibly strong women in my life. I never lacked for guidance and love, even when I didn't want either of the aforementioned.

When Hugh located me, I was shocked, but I knew he was telling the truth about who he was when Atti all but turned him into a bullfrog the moment I opened the door. If my father hadn't blocked his spell, I shudder to think what the aftermath would have been.

Also, we look a bunch alike. There's no denying Hugh's my father. All in all, he's really a good guy, if not vain and almost comically superficial.

To say there's no love lost between my father and Atti is an understatement. However, meeting him led me to find my sister, Stevie, who's technically my half-sister (my dad was a busy, busy guy in the romance department), but I couldn't be more pleased to still have a relative I can count on if things get tough. My life has become so much richer for having Stevie in it, and her familiar, Belfry.

Anyway, my uncle's whimsical, devil-may-care nature never sat well with my hummingbird familiar, and he hasn't a single qualm about sharing his displeasure.

"Listen, Atti, if not for that fling Uncle Darling encouraged Mom to have, you wouldn't have me. Are you saying you'd rather she didn't have a summer romance and didn't end up knocked up by the famous-only-in-Japan star of stage, screen, and TV, Hugh Granite?" I teased.

He pecked at my ponytail with his long beak before landing on my shoulder. "Don't be so crass, Halliday," he drawled. "She was not knocked up. She became impregnated by a two-bit, D-list actor who happens to look like Cary Grant and Rock Hudson all rolled into one vain, muscled package. Of course I'm not saying that. I'm saying, your Andrew encourages poor behavior. That's what I'm saying. I worry he'll encourage you to do the same."

I grinned. "So you think I'm going to have a summer romance and get knocked up because Uncle Darling's here? It's winter, in case you hadn't noticed. Too cold for a fling—no matter what Uncle Darling says."

"Says you. How quickly we've forgotten your gentleman caller, Hobbs."

I sighed, maybe a little too breathy to hide. I liked Hobbs. I liked him a lot. I liked that he rented the cottage behind my house and I liked his dog, Stephen King. But I really liked that we'd spent a lot of time together since we were almost killed last week.

I know that sounds a little off-kilter, but we'd bonded over having to run for our lives. In fact, we'd spent a good portion of our days together since, sharing meals, and decorating, and talking about everything from my life in New York as an interior designer to his prior job as a financial advisor.

"He's not fling material, my funny feathered friend. Hobbs is a fine Southern gentleman who's never been anything other than respectful."

"As he should be, or I shall turn him into something dreadful like a gargoyle or a hedgehog."

"Do gargoyle's really exist, Atti?"

"I've seen many things in my time, Halliday. I'm certain I've seen one or two."

"Your time as in when the dinosaurs roamed the earth?" I teased.

He scoffed. "Aren't you quite practiced for your stint at the comedy club performing standup, Miss Witch?"

My phone beeped a text then, and I grabbed it off the counter to see if it was from Uncle Darling. In my haste, I almost knocked over the mini Christmas tree I'd just placed next to a long wooden dough bowl filled with greenery and ornaments. I'd begun to worry. The roads were probably a mess of ice and visibility was undoubtedly low.

Also, Uncle Darling really was a hideous driver.

Atticus hadn't been kidding. I hoped Monty had taken the wheel.

As I began to read, my eyes went wide and I had to grab ahold of the countertop, letting the cold quartz ease my suddenly hot palms.

I gasped. This was bad. This was so bad.

"Holy—"

"Uh-uh-uh," Atti warned, cutting off my penchant for using foul language as he landed on the island counter. "Halliday? What's wrong, Poppet?"

"Stiles… he just texted me on Uncle Darling's phone. It's Monty," I barely murmured, my head swimming.

"What is it? Did that wanker land in a snowbank? It's just as I told you, Halliday, that man is treacherous behind the wheel of a car. He shouldn't be allowed to drive a remote for a battery-operated car, let alone four thousand pounds of steel on icy roads."

I squeezed my temples before texting him back and shoving my phone into my back pocket, looking for my jacket and my hat and gloves. I ran to our long walnut-stained dining room table next to the fireplace and grabbed my jacket from the back of a chair.

"Halliday? What is happening? You have me quite worried! Answer me, please!"

Pulling on my coat and hat, I dug in my jacket for my gloves. "It's Monty. He's been hurt, Atti. Uncle Darling's at the convenience store just outside of town. I have to go get him. He's hysterical."

"What happened?"

"Murder..." I whispered.

"What, child? Another one? Isn't it rather early in the season for another murder after we've only just had one last week?"

I licked my dry lips, my only concern getting to Uncle Darling, who never handled a crisis well. "I've got to go, Atti, and yes, I'll be safe. I promise. But I have to go get him. According to Uncle Darling, someone murdered Gable Norton—and Monty saw it happen!"

CHAPTER 2

Baby, It's Cold Outside
    Written by Frank Loesser, Henry D. Haynes,
Jethro Burns, 1944

I flew out the door and into the garage, beeping my truck, climbing in, and pressing the garage door open.

As I began to back out, Hobbs was suddenly directly behind me in my rearview mirror, making me slam on the brakes. He came to the window and knocked on it, his handsome face concerned, his knit cap covered in snow.

I pressed the button to roll down the window. "You scared the devil out of me!"

"Hal? What's goin' on? I was just taking out my garbage and saw your taillights. Everythin' okay?" he asked, his Southern accent thicker when he was worried. "It's stormin' pretty hard out."

"Remember I told you about my Uncle Darling coming to visit with his husband Monty this week?"

He grinned then, making his beard lift and the deep grooves on either side of his mouth more pronounced. "I do. I was looking forward to meeting 'em. Is everything all right?"

"I have to go get him. He's at the convenience store just outside of town. His husband's been hurt—and apparently, the convenience store clerk was killed, and Monty witnessed it."

Hobbs blinked, but he didn't miss a beat. "You okay to drive?"

I gripped the steering wheel. "I'm fine. I grew up here, remember? This is like a walk in the park for me."

"If you don't object, I'll come with you. Call me a typical man...that is to say, I'm sure you can handle drivin' in this blizzard just fine, but I'd like to go with you to be sure. Doesn't mean I don't trust your abilities as a driver. I know you don't need a man to drive in the snow. Just means I don't wanna see you out on that dark country road all alone."

I couldn't help but smile. It didn't upset me that Hobbs wanted to look out for me. Not even a little, as long as he tacked on that little part where he acknowledged I was okay doing it alone.

Still, he was right. Though it was only late afternoon, it was already dark on that short stretch of road from town to the convenience store. Dark and deserted.

"Make no mistake, this isn't a blizzard, Texas Man. It's a squall, but by all means, hop in. I appreciate the company."

He rounded the back of the vehicle and climbed in, the scent of wet snow and his fresh cologne invading the interior of my truck.

Hobbs turned to me and gave me a warm, sympathetic smile. "So what's going on? How can I help?"

I handed him my phone. "Read the texts from my uncle."

He was quiet for a moment as I backed out of the driveway and plowed forward into the snowy night. Flipping on my satellite radio, I chose the Christmas station and turned it low, letting the dulcet tones of Bing Crosby soothe me.

But my stomach was in a jumble of nerves. I wasn't sure what I was going to walk into. The last crime scene I'd witnessed, I saw from a distance. Having a personal stake in it took it to a whole new level.

"Wow," Hobbs mumbled. "He sounds pretty freaked out."

I nodded, navigating the small twists and turns in the road. "He is, and I'm going to warn you, he's pretty dramatic on the whole. I love him, but he takes embellishing to a new height. So I'm hoping maybe Gable isn't dead and this is all just a scratch or something, because the sight of blood makes my uncle go weak in the knees."

"I hate to tell you this, but he did say he saw someone running away and that Gable is dead. Maybe it's no exaggeration."

But I could still hope it was Uncle Darling being Uncle Darling—flamboyant, sarcastic, and more flamboyant. As we rounded the final bend to the convenience store, I saw the flash of red and blue lights and wondered if Stiles was actually there.

He'd soothe my uncle with his familiar face, but I couldn't remember his schedule these days. I felt like lately, he was always working to prove some point to that sourpuss Detective Godfrey.

I slowed to a crawl and parked on the side of the road, the lights in the convenience store—plus the ambulance and police car flashers—bright enough for us to walk the rest of the way.

Hobbs was out of the truck before I could blink, pulling open my door and offering me his gloved hand to help me down.

He leaned in and whispered in my ear, "I don't think he was exaggerating."

Nodding, my words were shaky when I whispered back, "I think you're right."

The convenience store loomed in front of me, a box-shaped structure of neon signs for beer and soft drink companies, with a red tin roof and a newspaper stand.

As we clomped through the snow, I heard my Uncle and his hysterical sobs while someone was carried off on a gurney and someone else shouted orders before loading whoever was on the gurney into the ambulance.

"Hal!" I heard Stiles call to me, and caught sight of him behind the crowd of police and forensics team members, his arms raised high. "Over here!"

I held a hand over my eyes to keep the flakes from pounding my face and crunched across the parking lot with Hobbs leading the way, noting the huge drops of blood as we got closer to the store.

Feeney's Fuel and Gruel, owned by Lamont Feeney, had been around since I was a kid. We used to ride our bikes here in the summer to buy ice cream and chips or a soda, because Feeney's always had the best ice cream —the word according to Stiles.

Mr. Feeney made a point of stocking Bomb Pops for Stiles the minute he'd found out he liked them, and he still did to this day. But the best thing about Feeney's was the lobster roll sandwiches—or if you're a local, the lobstah rolls.

Weird for a gas station to have them, I know, but he made the best lobster roll in all of Marshmallow Hollow.

That he'd managed not to end up bought out by a bigger corporation was admirable. Though, he had turned the management of the store over to Gable Norton last year, when Gable came home from rehab and needed a job. Mr. Feeney worked with all sorts of folks who had substance abuse problems at the church in town, because he's a recovering alcoholic himself.

So when Gable cleaned up, Mr. Feeney was the first

person to extend a hand to help him get on his feet. I hated thinking he was dead after he'd come so far…

I waved to Stiles and pushed my way around the sidewalk toward him, and that's when my uncle saw me and fairly collapsed against my chest.

"Oh, Hal!" he cried, using my scarf to wipe his tears. "Oh, Lamb, it's dreadful. Just dreadful! He's…he's going to die! Monty's going to die!"

Stiles was on hand to help me lead my uncle into the bright interior of the store, where it was warmer. "Don't move from this spot, Hal. Okay? They're still processing the crime scene, but they've taken Monty to the hospital."

"How bad it is?" I mouthed to him over my uncle's chubby shoulder.

"Bad," Stiles mouthed back, his handsome face, red from the cold and very grim, making me gulp and force myself to gather my wits in order to be strong for Uncle Darling.

Hobbs came in behind me and stood at my back, his hand on my waist, but he remained silent as my uncle cried and we both absorbed the mess the store had become.

Everything mostly looked the way it had when I was a kid, from the rows of candy and chips and a small selection of sundries, to the coolers with beer and soda.

Apparently there'd been a scuffle, because the shelves closer to the bathroom were knocked over, cans of coffee and small jugs of laundry detergent scattered across the floor. The rack that held fresh flowers from the local flower shop, where you could grab a small bouquet of carnations, was toppled over, green leaves everywhere.

And those drops of blood were all over the place, too—from the cashier's counter all the way to the bathrooms down a short hallway. I didn't know if they were from Monty or Gable or both, but seeing them made me shiver.

"Nooo!" I heard a female voice scream, raw and ragged. "No! No! No! Please, say it's not true, Stiles! Please tell me he's not gone!"

Blanching, I realized Gable's wife, Anna, had arrived, and hearing her cry out could only mean Gable was dead for sure.

Uncle Darling lifted his head, his wide blue eyes brimming with tears, his raspy voice cracking. "We need to get to Monty, Hal. They wouldn't let me go in the ambulance. I absolutely must go to him. He's the love of my life. I can't lose him! Not now!"

Hugging him hard, I cupped his cheeks and forced him to look at me. "Listen to me, Uncle Darling, I have to be sure you're allowed to leave. So I need you to take a deep breath and answer my question. Do you know if the police have any more questions for you?"

He gripped my wrists, his pudgy face collapsing. "I don't know, but I have to go to him, Hal. He needs me!"

Wiping his tears with my gloved fingers, like he'd done for me so many times, I nodded. "I understand, and I'll get you to him as soon as I can. I swear I will.

But first, let me check with Stiles, all right? I know it's hard, but we can't just run off if they need to talk to you. Okay?"

"O...okay," he sobbed, raspy and deep as he clung to my arms.

"I've got him, Hal," Hobbs said, and I gratefully mouthed my thanks.

Planting a kiss on my Uncle Darling's wet cheek, I pointed to Hobbs. "This is Hobbs, he's renting the cottage behind me and he's a friend. Is it okay if he stays with you while I check to see what needs to be done?"

Now, if you knew anything at all about my uncle, you'd know Hobbs would certainly warrant a slick comment about how good-looking he was, but my uncle didn't make a single off-color remark.

Instead, when Hobbs held out his hand, he went directly to him, his head low, his tears splotching the white tiled floor.

Hobbs pulled him away from me and back toward the beer cases, speaking to him in soothing tones.

I waved Stiles over, my nerves feeling a little frazzled. As he approached, the crisp legs on the pants of his uniform wet at the ankles, his face looked positively green.

Reaching out a hand, I grabbed his wrist. I didn't know if he was friends with Gable in school, he'd been a year behind us, and if I'm truthful, back in the day, he'd been a terrible bully.

It didn't seem likely that Stiles would have been friends with him, but he sure looked pretty upset.

"You okay, Fitzi?" I asked, calling him by his nickname when I tugged on his police-issued jacket.

"I'm okay, Kitten. Seeing Anna like that was tough. They have a baby, and I gotta say, it was pretty awful to see her so torn up."

I caught sight of Anna on the other side of the convenience store, where the police were huddled around her, giving me only a glimpse of her beautiful blonde hair and her face, red from crying.

I bit the inside of my cheek at the tragedy of it all. She'd just had a little girl a couple of months ago. In fact, Gable had been showing the baby's picture to anyone who'd look when they came into the store.

"Gosh, that's awful." I rubbed his arm. "So what in blazes happened here? Uncle Darling's beside himself over Monty."

Stiles blew out a breath. "I'm not sure of the details because Darling was hysterical and there was no calming him down. I think, and I use that word loosely, that Monty came in to use the facilities and grab you some flowers because he insisted, in Darling's words, they be fresh for his favorite little witch. Monty took too long, so Uncle Darling decided to come looking for him, and someone in a knit mask ran out of the bathroom, almost knocking him down. He ran to the bathroom to find Monty covered in blood and unconscious, and Gable shot...*dead*."

My stomach jolted. How awful for Uncle Darling.

"So that was Monty being taken away in the ambulance?"

I know it was a dumb question to ask, it definitely wasn't Gable on the gurney, but I almost needed to hear it out loud to digest the information.

He gave me a curt nod, gulping hard. "It was, and it looks pretty serious, Hal. I won't hesitate to say I'm worried about him."

Crap, crap, and more crap. "Okay, so can we take Darling to the hospital to see what's happening? Or does he have to answer more questions?"

"How about I go check and I'll get back to you in a sec. There's a lot going on."

I'd say. The team of forensic people were in and out of the small hallway leading to the men's bathroom, their faces somber, plastic on their shoes, leaving bloody footprints in their wake.

No less than four police officers and Detective Godfrey were talking to Anna, and that didn't even account for the other police officers outside, marking off the parking lot.

"Yes, please go check," I whispered, my heart pounding as Anna began to cry again, her husky sobs agonizing to hear.

A female police officer came and took hold of her, escorting her to a car outside, her arm around Anna's shoulders, keeping her close.

Thankfully, the car drove away, and I was glad for it...because what happened next will probably haunt my dreams forever.

There were a couple of grunts from the back where the men's room was located and then, without warning, another gurney came out. Maybe someone hadn't covered Gable's body well enough or the sheet had slipped off, but I got a bird's eye view of my first murder victim.

Four sturdy men pushed the gurney carrying Gable, his brown eyes glassy and wide, his mouth in a thin line of what looked like pain, suggesting he'd experienced anguish at the hands of his killer.

But that wasn't the worst of it. The worst of it was the hole in his chest. From where I stood, it looked enormous and ragged, the tear in his Feeney's Fuel and Gruel shirt blackened around the edges.

My stomach flipped upside down as someone yelled, "Didn't I tell you to wait until I cleared everyone out, you idiots? Have some respect and cover him up!"

As they passed Uncle Darling, I heard him cry out a primal scream seconds before the ground beneath me began to swell and lift—and with no warning, I was in the men's bathroom of Feeney's, watching two men fight for control of a shotgun while Monty lie on the small tiles of the bathroom floor.

Crumpled, almost broken, his slender face slack, his glossy red hair bloodied.

My heartbeat slowed, and as though my feet were made of concrete, rooted to the spot, I watched the split second play out when Gable Norton had fought for his life.

CHAPTER 3

Oh, Holy Night
  Written by Adolphe Adam, Placide Cappeau, John Sullivan Dwight, 1847

For sure, one man was Gable; I'd know his towhead and hulking frame anywhere. At one time, he'd been the golden boy of Marshmallow Hollow, the star quarterback at our high school (go Chickadees!), and all the girls had wanted him to take notice of them. Even though he'd been a year behind me, he'd played varsity football, and being a bit of a football fan when I was in school, I saw him play at most of the games.

The other man, just as Uncle Darling had told Stiles, definitely had a black knit facemask on, but he wasn't nearly as large as Gable. He was average height but broad-shouldered. They were shouting at one another, but the words were as muffled and hazy as my heartbeat.

They tussled for a moment and, of all the curious things, a tube of lipstick fell on the ground near Monty. A tube of hot-pink lipstick with no cap…

Then there was a loud boom and then blood everywhere.

Dear Goddess, the blood…

"Hal!" someone hissed with urgency in my ear. "Hal, listen to me. You're having a vision. I'm going to grab your hand to keep you steady. Come back to the land of the living."

I blinked, my eyes dry from the forced-air heat of the store, my legs wobbly and weak.

"Hal? You okay?"

I gripped what turned out to be Stiles's hand and nodded with a slow nod. "Yes…"

"What did you see?"

I leaned against his chest for a moment. He's a good deal taller than me, and my head only reaches his pecs. "The murderer, I think…I think I saw…the guy who murdered Gable."

His grip on me tightened as the world came back into focus. "*Who*? Who was it, Hal?"

"I don't know," I murmured in frustration. "I don't mean I *saw him*-saw him, you know? But it was just like Uncle Darling said, there was a man in a black knit facemask, and a tube of…lipstick? Hot-pink lipstick. What does that mean? Was it Uncle Darling's?"

He was, after all, a drag queen. He had tons of lipstick. In fact, he'd showed me how to contour my cheekbones and make my lips look fuller. He rarely traveled with his makeup if he wasn't on tour or doing a show, but I suppose it was possible he or even Monty had it.

Stiles shook his head and rasped a sigh. "I don't know, I didn't see the scene directly, and I haven't heard anything about a lipstick, but I'm sure if there is one, they'll ask Uncle Darling about it. Guaranteed. Anything else?"

Sighing, I scrunched my eyes shut and popped them back open. "I don't have much more than what he already told you. I'm sorry…"

We'd had a long conversation about the last murder I'd kind of infringed on, and the visions I'd had associated with said murder, and we'd agreed that my visions could have been helpful in solving the crime. If Stiles couldn't reveal what I told him to his superiors, at the very least he could be aware of what I'd seen and keep a keen eye open when looking for clues.

I know he had to be careful about any details he shared, and I didn't ever want him to jeopardize his work, but I did promise to share any future visions I had with him in case they could help.

Stiles patted me on the back and dropped a kiss on the top of my head. "Don't be sorry. I'm used to half the story when it comes to your *migraines*," he said. "But if you have another one with more clarity, text me, okay?"

I pushed off from his chest and nodded, my breathing returning to normal.

"She okay? Another migraine?" Brett Messer—tall and lanky with brown hair and pleasant hazel eyes— asked as he braced his hands on the heavy belt that held his gun.

Brett was two years older than us, and he'd lived in Marshmallow Hollow all his life—he was aware of my "debilitating migraines."

I held up a hand. "She is. Thanks for asking, Brett." Turning to Stiles, I asked, "Can I take Uncle Darling to the hospital now, or do you need him for more questioning?"

"You're good to go, and I'm sure I don't need to say this, but tell him not to leave Marshmallow Hollow."

I rolled my eyes. "As if he'd ever in a mill leave Monty."

Now Stiles held up his hands in defense of his words. "I'm just doing my job, Kitten. I gotta go, but I'll check on you guys later, okay?"

Taking a deep breath, I gave him a thumb's up before I went to gather Uncle Darling and Hobbs and head to the hospital.

But before I did, I sent out a small prayer to the universe.

Please, please let Monty be all right.

Please.

"We should have stayed at the hospital and waited, Hal," Uncle Darling sobbed forlornly over a cup of his favorite hot tea Atticus had all prepared as soon as we'd walked in the door. "No! Instead, I should do a healing spell and make it all go away with the snap of my fingers!"

I reached for his chubby fingers and gripped them, pulling his fist to my cheek. "You know you can't do that, Uncle Darling. We mustn't interfere with mortal matters, and Uncle Monty is mortal."

His round face sagged as tears rimmed his eyes again. "You're right, Lamb. I know you're right, but... I should have stayed with him—waited for him. *Healed* him."

Monty had a hematoma from a blow to his head. I'm not sure if the man in the mask hit him, or he hit his head on the stall in the bathroom, but they had to relieve the pressure on his brain, and that meant surgery and possibly an induced coma to hopefully bring the swelling down.

The prognosis at this point was iffy, and I was doing my best not to show Uncle Darling how terrified I really was.

Uncle Darling had been beside himself when Doc Jordan had told him the news, but Hobbs had managed to convince him to come back to the house and at least try to rest.

Hobbs had gone home to grab Stephen King and take him out, and was due back at any moment, but he'd been an enormous help in soothing my distraught Darling.

I rubbed his back and pressed another tissue into his hands, planting a kiss on his round cheek. "You know you can't interfere with fate. Healing him is out of the question, and you heard what Doctor Jordan said, Uncle Darling. Monty's going to be in surgery for a while. There's nothing we can do right now. It's much better if we wait here for the text from the staff nurse when surgery is over than watch you pace a hole in the floor and drive yourself crazy with worry. You can't be with him right now, so it's better you're here with me— with us. He's in good hands, and so are you, I promise."

With a shudder, he took a sip of his tea as another tear rolled down his face. "Thank you for this, Atticus. I'm gagged you'd think of me."

"Gagged?" Atticus twittered, settling on the island counter. "Is this some sort of drag queen speak, Andrew?"

Giving Atti a stern look, I shook my head to let him know now wasn't the time to pick at Uncle Darling's slang.

"In pretentious British speak, it means he's gobs-macked, Atti. It's a nice thing. Now hush with all that Brits-do-it-best snobbery."

"*Gagged*," Atticus scoffed. "What has happened to the English language? We've all but trampled it to death. Who's happy to be gagged, I ask?"

I glared at Atti, reminding him yet again this wasn't the time, and he was ruining the perfectly warm feelings he'd created by being kind enough to have tea prepared for us when we walked in the door.

Uncle Darling, unperturbed by Atti, grabbed my hand, his deep brown eyes searching mine. "Does that walking, talking, bearded fantasy know about you, Sweet Face?"

That was more like my uncle than he'd been all night. "Nope. We've only known each other a little while. I'm not ready to share yet. But he *has* witnessed a vision."

He sniffled and dabbed at his eyes with the tissue. "Still calling your visions 'migraines'?"

I gripped his hand and gazed into his swollen eyes. "I am, and that's what Hobbs thinks they are, too. For the moment, that's enough."

"Tell me about him, Hal," Uncle Darling demanded. "Take my mind off the sheer torture of waiting for the hospital to call."

Grabbing my beer, I took a swig and tried to focus. "He's my tenant. He rents the cottage in back. He was some kind of financial advisor in Boston, but he's from Texas, an oddball Southern boy who loves the cold and the snow. After coming here on a daytrip with a friend, he decided to move here when he left his job."

Uncle Darling gasped, injecting his brand of drama as he placed his hand over his heart. "He has no job, Sugarbuns? How does he pay his bills? You're not letting him freeload, are you?"

I smiled. "I think he made a lot of money and retired really early. I've never had a check bounce, and he's been here full time for a couple of months. No freeloading, though I might let him have the place if he'd let me have his dog, Stephen King."

He patted my hand and nodded. "Well, he's a dish, isn't he? Or trade, as we'd call him in the drag business."

Listen, I've watched a lot of *RuPaul's Drag Race* in honor of my Uncle Darling so we could talk about it when we chatted on the phone, but I didn't know what trade meant.

I squinted at him. "Er, trade? Do I want to know what that means?"

He gave me his coy-sly smile, one of his specialties, and said, "The meaning's evolved some, but when I use it, it means I wouldn't look the other way if he were interested in some hanky-panky. More or less, anyway."

Giggling, I wagged a finger at him. "I don't think I want to know what more or less means. Either way, he's a nice guy and—"

"And he likes our Halliday. They've been together ever since they were chased down by a deranged killer with a gun last week." Atti buzzed upward toward the top of the mini Christmas tree and seated himself on a branch.

"*What?*" Uncle Darling yelped, jumping up from the stool at the counter, a frown on his face. "If your mother were here, she'd positively hold my feet to the fire for allowing you to be in any danger!"

I put my hands on his shoulders and sat him back

down. "I'm a grown woman, and I couldn't help the danger. It's a long story, Uncle Darling. Suffice it to say, we made a discovery together we didn't want to make and that discovery had a big, bad gun."

"And a vicious attack dog Halliday turned into a giraffe," Atticus pointed out in his deep voice.

Now Darling sputtered. "Oh, Lamb Chop, no. A giraffe?" he squealed.

I frowned and hung my head, driving my hands into the pockets of my jeans. "Yeah. Unfortunately, Atti's right. I used my magic to get us out of a sticky situation, but you know how fluky it can be when I'm anything but calm. Things got a little out of control."

Glancing at his phone, Uncle Darling sighed. "You and your out-of-control magic. It was your mother's biggest worry. Remind me to introduce you to some calming techniques when this is…over." And then his eyes filled with more tears.

I wrapped an arm around his shoulder and rested my head on it, sniffing the scent of laundry detergent. "I love you, and it's going to be all right, Uncle Darling. I feel it."

I didn't know if that was true—if I felt Uncle Monty was going to be all right—but I also didn't know what else to say. The only thing I did know? I wish my mother were here. She'd know what to say. She always knew what to say.

Swiping at his eyes, he dropped an angry fist to the countertop. "I should have never let him talk me into stopping, Hal. He insisted on bringing you flowers—

you know how much he loves you. But like everything with Monty, they had to be perfect. Except that blessed fool wouldn't listen when I told him Feeney's would have nothing but carnations, and absolutely nothing that lived up to his standards. He insisted I stop, and because I love him more than my own life, I did." He inhaled then and let out a wail of distress. "Why didn't I ignore him, Hal? Why? I was driving. I should have listened to my gut. I knew it was a bad idea. I knew it!"

The guilt I felt about those flowers was enough to make my chest tight and my heart throb erratically, and I'm guessing uncle Darling picked up on that because he instantly pulled me into a tight hug.

He wrapped his beefy arms around me and nuzzled my nose with his. "I'm sorry, Lovey," he whispered against my hair, his body shuddering. "This has nothing to do with you. I didn't mean to hurt your feelings."

I knew that logically, but my heart ached anyway. "I know that rationally. I do, but it doesn't change the fact that he was trying to do something nice for me. I love Uncle Monty. You know I do. He means the world to me," I said, leaning back in his beefy arms.

Brushing my hair from my eyes, he gave me a watery smile. "I know that, Lamb. He loves you, too."

Then I gathered myself. I had to know what my vision meant, and while I wasn't ready to tell my uncle I'd had one involving Monty and the killer yet, I needed to try and understand what I'd seen.

In the meantime, knowing he likely hadn't eaten, I

snapped my fingers and produced a plate of apple strudel, Uncle Darling's favorite, ignoring the frown from Atti's direction.

As he reached for some, and Atti produced a fork and plate, I ventured into the shallow end of the pool. "Listen, Uncle Darling, can you tell me what you remember? I know it's painful, but maybe I can help."

Sitting back down, he grimaced. "How can you possibly help, Lamb?"

I shrugged, downplaying my interest. "I dunno. You'd be surprised, but the saying two heads are better than one is really true. So what happened?"

His breath shuddered from his chest as he shivered. I snapped my fingers again and a warm shawl appeared around his shoulders. He gave me a grateful smile and tucked it around his rotund body.

"I don't know where to begin, Sugar, but I'll try. Like I told those police officers and my sweet boy Stiles, we stopped to get flowers. I stayed in the car because I didn't want to haul my big fanny through the snow. I had my earbuds in, and I was listening to some new music from a fellow drag sister, Helen Highwater, so I wasn't really paying attention to anything. Monty was taking forever and a day, and if you know anything about my man, you'll know he's like molasses uphill in the winter. So I decided to check on him. I was gonna give him all sorts of what for, and then...then..."

He set the fork for the strudel down and let his chin fall to his chest.

I grabbed his hand and squeezed it for support. "I

know this is hard, but did you see anything while you were in the car, Uncle Darling? Did you see the person who killed Gable go inside?"

His sigh was ragged and he covered his mouth to muffle a sob, but he shook his head. "It was snowing like somebody'd dumped a box of instant mashed potato flakes on our heads. But I also had my eyes closed while I listened to the music." He shook his head. "I didn't see anyone go inside. I didn't even see the car he was driving, Hal. I should have paid better attention."

"So he was driving a car? Are you sure? If you had your eyes closed, how do you know?"

"When he ran past me to get out of Feeney's, I saw him get into one. I *know* I did," he insisted.

My heart began to throb all over again. "Did you see what kind of car it was?"

His round face went slack with frustration under the glow of the twinkling lights in the kitchen. "Aw, Lamb, you know I don't know cars from a hole in the wall. Now ask me about a brand of makeup, or a dress designer, and you can't get me to shut my pretty mouth. The only thing I can tell you is it was an older car, without all the finery of the newer models. It was a sedan, maybe dark green."

Blowing out a breath of air, I reminded myself this might take some patience. "Why does that make you think it was an older car, Uncle Darling?"

"Because it looked dull and rusty, I guess. I don't know! By then, I was so stunned, so shaking in my pantaloons, I thought I might pass out, Hal. He had a gun. A big, long gun. I had no idea he'd just shot a hole the size of the sun in someone with it!"

His agitation began to make me uneasy and worried. When Uncle Darling gets going, there's nothing to do but ride out the spiral. I couldn't afford for him to spiral now.

"I should have zapped that man when I saw him running from the bathroom! Why didn't I zap him, Lamb?"

Boy, did I know that question well. I also knew the answer. "Because you were scared, Uncle Darling. You can't blame yourself," I soothed.

"I froze! That's why," he almost howled. "It's so unlike me, but I froze as sure as I'm standing here!"

"Andrew!" Atticus belted out, his deep voice reverberating around the kitchen as he buzzed in front of Uncle Darling's face. "You will gather yourself this instant. There will be no meltdowns in my presence. Hal is trying to help you find the person who caused undue harm to your beloved, and we must help get justice for him. Answer the questions and do it like an adult!"

Uncle Darling instantly sat up straighter, even if he glared at Atticus. "I'm sorry, Lamb. You know how wound up I can get."

I rubbed his back with the flat of my palm and dropped a kiss on his cheek. "I do, but I need you to hold it together for just a little bit, please. Now, let's see what we can figure out, okay? You said you went inside. Was the killer still inside when you went to check on Uncle Monty?"

He swallowed hard and nodded with a violent shiver. "Yes. I heard them fighting and then...the... gunshot. He came running out just after I came into the store, and he had that gun in his hand, and it was so big, Lamb. I've never seen one up close, and I was so terrified, but he paid no mind to me. He just ran out of the store. He'd obviously killed that poor child just after I got into the store, but I don't understand what happened to Monty. I just don't understand how he managed not to get himself shot."

"Did the killer see you, Uncle Darling?" That sent a shiver of unadulterated fear along my spine.

"I don't know if he saw me, but it doesn't matter if I saw him because he had on a ski mask. A black, knit ski mask. He was dressed in *all* black. In fact, he was very chic, something I'd envy if he hadn't slaughtered that poor boy and hurt my Monty."

What an odd thing to stand out, but Uncle Darling was like my sister, in that fashion was very important in both their lives, unlike me, who really loved a good flannel shirt and a pair of jeans.

"Chic? How do you mean, he was chic?"

"I know this sounds absolutely crackers for me to have noticed something so random and trivial in light of the fact that I was petrified, but I noticed his trousers were clean and pleated down the front to within an inch of their life. Once a fashionista, always a fashionista, I suppose. Even in the killing fields of Feeney's."

"Can you remember any other details like that? Did he say anything? Did you hear anything?"

That was when Uncle Darling almost jumped off the chair, his aging eyes wide. "Hold on...just hold on! I *did* hear him say something." He put his fingers to his temples and squeezed.

I held my breath and waited as Atticus asked urgently, "What did he say, Andrew?"

Rolling up the sleeves of his heavy red sweater, he winced. "He said...give me that stupid S..." He paused a moment and bunched his fist in front of his mouth as though he were thinking, and then he yelled, "That SD card! Yes! He said give me that—pardon my colorful language—'effin' SD card.'"

Everyone grew quiet until Uncle Darling asked, "What in all of a Gucci bag is an SD card?"

I didn't know a lot about computers and tech, but I knew enough to know what an SD card was used for. But before I could answer...

"It's usually what stores the memory in a phone or a video surveillance camera."

CHAPTER 4

Underneath the Tree
Written by Kelly Clarkson, Greg Kurstin, 2013

---

*H*obbs's husky voice gave us the answer as Stephen King grunted his way into the kitchen and placed his thick paws on my thighs for some love. "What makes you ask?"

I'd told Hobbs to let himself in when he was done feeding and walking Stephen King. Somehow, his presence made the task of talking to Uncle Darling less daunting. He appeared to comfort him in a way I couldn't.

I smiled down at Stephen King and stooped to press a kiss on his broad tan and white head. "That's what the killer said when Uncle Darling first entered the store. Apparently, the killer was fighting with

Gable in the men's room, and if he wanted an SD card, he probably wanted to erase the video of him being there. The question is, why? I mean, sure, it's a good safeguard to keep from being identified, but he was masked, and I'd bet my life savings he covered his tracks."

Hobbs pulled off his rawhide jacket and knit cap, hanging them both on a chair in the dining room before he said, "Mind bringing me up to speed?"

I repeated what Uncle Darling had told us as I got him a beer and popped the top off, setting it in front of him on the kitchen counter. "And that's where we're at," I finished on a grim note.

Hobbs cleared his throat. "First, let me say my thoughts are with Monty, Andrew, and I'm here if you need anything at all."

Uncle Darling looked Hobbs in the eye and pointed a finger at him. "You, Mr. Dish of a Cowboy, can call me Uncle Darling, and thank you, Presh. You were a huge help to me at the store."

Hobbs tipped his beer at him in acknowledgement. "Second, what's up with the SD card? If he was disguised, why the heck would he want the video from the surveillance camera? That's a clue if I ever heard one."

Blowing out a breath, I shook my head. "Uncle Darling said he was dressed all in black, and he noticed creases in the pants of his trousers, but that doesn't feel like something that anyone could easily make an identification from. Maybe he had something else on him that could identify him, but Uncle Darling missed it? That's my best guess."

Hobbs cupped his bearded chin. "And here's something else, why would a guy who was going to commit a crime in a raging snowstorm wear dressy pants, and not boots or snow gear?"

"Is there a fashion rule against wearing dressy clothes to commit a crime?" I asked. "Like a dress code amongst criminals?"

"Still hopin' to kickstart that standup career, huh, Hal?" Hobbs asked with a laugh. Then he shrugged, his wide shoulders lifting under his white-and-blue-checked flannel shirt. "I just mean, it's dadgum cold out there at thirteen degrees. What criminal wears dress pants anyway? Maybe it has something to do with who he is or what he does when he's not committing murder. Just stuck out to me."

Wincing, I clenched my fists together when I remembered Gable's body being carried off to the ambulance. "You have a point, let's put that away for now because I have another question."

I had to be careful how I asked this. I didn't want to lie to Hobbs about how I knew, but I guess I really didn't have a choice. There's never been another human soul I've told about my magic.

In fact, if you're wondering, I never even told my ex-fiancé, and even though I could never figure out why I wasn't entirely honest, now I'm glad I wasn't.

Our breakup was ugly, and he was angry that I'd left him with nothing but the bed he'd cheated on me in.

He sent me ugly texts for a long time after. Imagine how that would have gone, had he the kind of ammunition knowing I was a witch would give him.

The only two humans who know are Stiles and Uncle Monty, and I didn't know how long it would be before I could tell Hobbs—or if I ever would. I needed complete trust, and that took time.

Yet, if I wanted his help... If I wanted him to help me figure out who'd hurt Uncle Monty, and if this person was out there lurking around, looking to shut him up entirely because he might have information that could identify the killer, I had to reveal everything I knew.

"Uncle Darling, did you or Monty have any lipstick on you tonight? Pink, specifically?" I knew the forensics team was going to find it, and if my vision was inaccurate, I'd make something up. But I had to know.

He flapped his hands at me, still looking miserable. "Not a stitch of makeup, Lamb. Nothing. I'm on the sauce when it comes to anything drag. It's been a nice break since I retired. And of course Monty wants nothing to do with makeup. He's a lighting engineer. He likes sounds systems and stage lights, not foundation and eyeshadow. Why do you ask?"

Shrugging, I pretended it was no big deal. "I heard one of the officers mention they'd found one, I think. Could be a customer dropped it. No big deal."

"Dropped it in the *men's* bathroom?" Hobbs asked.

I turned my face away and went to find a plate of the cookies I knew Hobbs liked and a treat for Stephen

King, to keep from looking him in the eye. Food always quieted Hobbs—especially cookies.

"Did I say it was in the men's bathroom? No. I did not." Crud. I'm a really bad liar. "And why can't a man have lipstick?"

"I'm not at all sayin' a man can't, but no matter the killers gender, it still could mean the killer dropped it," Hobbs suggested, not appearing to notice my irritability.

I put the white plate of cookies down in front of him and agreed. "Maybe so. But if we go with the law of averages, and he was a man, he wouldn't likely have a lipstick. I thought it seemed more likely Uncle Darling would have it, or maybe Monty was carrying it for him. That was where my train of thought was going."

Uncle Darling rolled his eyes. "Wouldn't it be ironic if he's a drag queen like me—or a cross-dresser...or a very sturdily-built woman?"

"Are you sure the person you saw was a man, Uncle Darling?"

He shuddered again, rubbing his hands over his arms when he looked to Hobbs with his answer. "I'm pretty sure, Good-Lookin'."

Grabbing my uncle by the hand, I pulled him upward. "C'mon. Let's go sit by the fire while we wait for news. It's beautiful by the fireplace and the tree is so pretty this year. The cowboy here helped decorate it."

I picked up his special Christmas mug, the one my

mother insisted we each have, with a picture of a snowman holding a gingerbread man's hand, and pulled him with me, tilting my head at Hobbs to encourage him to join us.

Uncle Darling stopped in front of the tree and said, "There's a light out in the middle of the tree, Lamb, shall I—"

I squeezed his hand and shook my head, reminding him with my eyes we were among mortals and he couldn't use his magic. "I'll fix it later. You shouldn't be worrying about anything but resting and having your tea."

Pulling an icy-white blanket with red pom-poms off the back of the couch, I turned on the sound system, piping some instrumental Christmas music through the house before leading him to a chair, covering him and dropping a kiss on his forehead.

But he held my hand tight when I tried to sit opposite him. "What if…" he asked, his voice trembling.

"What if you tell me how you became a drag queen?" Hobbs asked. "Ever since Hal told me about what you did for a living, I've been fascinated. I even watched some *RuPaul's Drag Race* in honor of your visit."

I smiled to myself. If there was anything Uncle Darling liked to do, it was talk about himself and his career, and Hobbs was very good at picking up on what made people tick.

A text buzzed from my phone in my back pocket, and when I pulled it out to see Stiles wanted me to call,

I decided it might be better to do so out of Uncle Darling's earshot.

"You guys mind if I go feed Karen? I didn't have time earlier, and I already know about how Uncle Darling clawed his way to the top and became the best lip-syncing eyeliner ninja in all the land."

My uncle blushed. Two bright spots appearing on his rounded cheeks, spots I was convinced he'd somehow taught himself to make appear when he wanted to come across as humble.

"Oh, you. It wasn't like that, Lamb, and you know it."

"Well, you tell Hobbs about your adventures while I go feed Na— Karen. I'll be right back." I plopped another kiss on the top of his head of thick hair.

As I left them, chatting amicably, Uncle Darling's hands animated, his voice less fraught with worry, I sighed a little. Hobbs was really good with people, and he was *really* good at making everyone around him feel comfortable.

Especially me.

Whistling to Atti, I trudged to the mudroom and pulled on my jacket and hat, pushing the door open to make my way to the barn. Atticus clung to my shoulder, nestling against the length of my hair to keep warm.

The bitter cold stung my eyes as the tang of the ocean crashing against the rocks settled in my lungs.

The barn wasn't far from the house, a big red structure with a loft and a few stalls. The way was lit with a million Christmas lights wrapped around the split-rail fencing and the mini arborvitae trees that bordered the path, but it was freezing, and that put some pep in my step.

Pulling out my phone as I pushed my way into the red door, I wandered over to my Nana. In case I haven't mentioned, my Nana Karen is reincarnated in a reindeer's body, and she's a handful, to say the least. To make everything that much more complicated, on top of her shenanigans, she talks.

Leaning down, I kissed the top of her velvety soft head. "Evening, Nana. How goes your night so far?"

She reared her head upward and nuzzled my hand. "Well, it'd be better if you had some candy canes."

I chuckled softly. "You know they're no good for your digestive system, Nana. It's not the same as a human's anymore. Also, they're high in sugar and Dr. Francine says no. So absolutely no candy canes."

"Dipsy doodles, you're a tyrant, Suzy Q," she groused at me.

Smiling, I stroked her head and straightened the harness on her back while I grabbed her some feed to fill her trough. "Just call me head tyrant. Now, other than that, how are you? Warm enough?"

"I'm not the one we need to be worrying for here, kiddo. How's Andrew and Monty?"

I looked up at the high ceiling and rasped out a sigh, the cold air puffing from my lips. "You heard?"

She bobbed her head and snuffed a snort. "Atti told

me. Poor boy. Just found the love of his life and now this."

I gulped and swallowed hard with a shiver. "Things aren't looking good, Nana. Monty's in surgery as we speak and Hobbs is with Uncle Darling, but I'm worried. I'm really worried about him," I said, my voice cracking. "I'm trying to keep it together for him, stay positive, but I'm scared."

"Hobbs'll fix Andrew right up. He could fix up the *Titanic*, that hottie could."

"Karen," Atti scolded in his deep voice. "The child is trying to keep her wits about her while supporting poor Andrew, whom, I might add, is a bloody wreck. Surely you have something more to comment on than the state of Hobbs's appearance."

"Atti's right. Shame on me. Sorry, sorry, sorry, honey. How can I help?"

Wrapping my arms around her, I gave her a tight hug she leaned into. "You can behave while he visits and we sort this mess out. That means no breaking out and running hog wild through town so I have to pick you up from animal control."

She stomped her hooves. "Anything for you, Sunshine. Tell your old nana what happened, while I eat, why don't ya?"

As I explained to her what Uncle Darling had witnessed and the details of Monty's surgery, I felt a little better. Talking to her always eased my mind— even if we didn't come to any conclusions or find any answers. It was just nice to be heard without the

47

restrictions of leaving my magic out of the conversation.

When I was finished, she said, "Yee-haw, kiddo. A second murder in just a few days? What the heck's goin' on 'round these parts? Poor Gable's wife and baby. Sure do feel sorry for 'em. You make sure you take somethin' to her, will ya?"

"Of course I will, Nana and I'll check to be sure they have enough to care for the new baby until she gets on her feet. Don't worry."

My phone buzzed again, reminding me why I'd come out to the barn in the first place.

"I have to call Stiles, Nana. But if you have any ideas about this mystery, you let me know. I'd welcome anything, because I'm fresh out."

With those words, I pressed my BFF's number.

Stiles picked up on the first ring. "Fitzsimmons," he answered curtly.

"Hey, Fitzi. You okay?"

"I'm okay. How's Uncle Darling and Monty?"

Tucking the phone under my chin, I grabbed the rake to muck Nana Karen's stall and give her some fresh hay. "Well, you know Uncle Darling. Still as dramatic as ever, but this time, he has good reason, and Uncle Monty..." My voice hitched before I took a deep breath. "He's not great." I explained what the doctor's said and that he was in surgery and, at this point, all we could do was hope.

There was a crackle on the phone line, a bit of static

before I heard his deep voice say, "I have a question for you."

His tone made my heart stop dead its tracks. I know Stiles almost as well as I know myself, and this was serious. "Okay, what's up?"

"That lipstick you saw in your vision?"

Stopping in front of Nana's stall, I stiffened. "What about it?"

"Where did you say you saw it again?"

Leaning back against the stall, I dragged a hand over my nana's head and smiled at her. "The men's bathroom at Feeney's. Why?"

"Secret squirrel?"

That meant I couldn't ever tell anyone, which was getting harder by the minute with Hobbs in my life. "I'm afraid to say yes, Stiles. You know Hobbs is in the thick of this, right? I already mentioned the lipstick to both Hobbs and Uncle Darling."

"Then you have to tell them secret squirrel, too, because I could get into a stink pile of trouble for this, Hal, but if you have another vision about the lipstick or anything, I need to know," he all but whispered in my ear.

I cocked my head, my stomach turning flips. "Stiles, we've been friends for a thousand years. I'd tell *my* secret before I'd tell one of yours. What's going on?"

There was a heavy pause and then he said, "That lipstick had fingerprints on it."

Blinking, I dropped the rake and inhaled with a sharp breath. "The killer's fingerprints?"

I heard him sigh and probably cup the phone with his hand to muffle his response. "No. The fingerprints of a seventeen-year-old girl who's been missing for *three days.*"

Oh, holy night...

CHAPTER 5

It's the Most Wonderful Time of the Year
    Written by Edward Pola and George Wyle, 1963

J gasped, realizing not only was the lipstick real, but that my vision had been more accurate than I'd first thought. "The fingerprints… Doesn't she have to be some kind of criminal to be in the system?"

At least that's what the explanation always was on one of my true-crime shows.

"She was in the system because of a background check for a position as a part-time babysitter. When I heard the forensics team did, in fact, find a lipstick and it had prints lifted from it, I asked what color it was, and it was for sure hot pink. Actually, it's called

Flamingo Flame, made by Christy of Paris, according to the label."

I gripped the phone tighter, my knees shaking. "Do you want me to ask Darling anything else about it? He said it isn't his. He claims he didn't bring any makeup with him this trip."

"He said the same thing to the cops on the scene."

"Wait. Uncle Darling knew about the lipstick?"

"No, Kitten. Because he was a drag queen, I asked him if he had one after I knew it was found, and he said he didn't have any makeup with him."

"So who's the girl, Stiles? Is it anyone we know?"

Dear Goddess, it was horrible that a girl was missing, but if we knew her… Though, that was unlikely. If she was someone missing from Marshmallow Hollow, I'd have heard about it.

"We don't know her. She's from Chester Bay."

The next town over. Chester Bay was bigger than Marshmallow Hollow by at least twenty thousand people, and not nearly as touristy. Though, most folks who wanted to experience my little town but couldn't book a room during the busy holiday season, often opted to stay in Chester Bay.

So close to home, it chilled my already chilled bones. "What's her name, Stiles? Can you tell me?"

"Secret squirrel again?"

"Till death."

"Kerry Carver. Last seen walking to the local bus stop from her after-school babysitting job three days ago. Her parents reported her missing, but as usual it got back-burnered because she hadn't been missing long. Even though, according to the report I got from Chester Bay's guys, her parents were adamant she always came home from work without fail. She wasn't, in their words, the kind of girl who stayed out late or partied."

My heart crashed against my ribs. This felt so close to home—so close. "Anything else?"

"Just that the shotgun the killer murdered Gable with might have been Mr. Feeney's. We finally located him and had him come to the store. He was understandably distraught, especially when he found out his gun is missing and it could be the one Gable was killed with."

"He kept a shotgun at the store? A *shotgun?*" I asked in surprise. I knew Mr. Feeney was a hunter, so were his sons, but I guess I never realized he kept a gun at the store.

Though, it made complete sense to have a gun at a convenience store—even in little old Marshmallow Hollow—because hello, Hannah, look at how many murders we'd had in just a few days.

"He did. He was licensed to carry, though in Maine, you don't need a permit to own one—or carry it, for that matter. But you know he and his boys loved to hunt in Iowa, and you need a permit to cross state lines with a gun."

Grimacing, I bit my lower lip. "I think you know my specialty is tinsel and talking Santas, not guns. So I didn't know that. But how did the killer get his hands on it?"

"I don't know. Though Mr. Feeney says Gable knew where it was and he had access to it. Our best guess is, Gable pulled the gun on the killer, but he wrestled it away from him in the fight that ensued, ending in the bathroom. And that's pretty much all I have."

I blew out a pent-up breath with a shiver. "Okay, so I have some info for you from Uncle Darling that's worth investigating. Did he say anything in his statement about the killer demanding an SD card? And have you looked at the store's surveillance tape yet?"

There was a moment of silence where I heard the sound of papers flipping, and then he said, "No. Nothing about an SD card. But, to be fair to Darling, he was in a state of total shock. Maybe more will come back to him as the night progresses. As to the video itself, I can't say for sure, but I *am* sure forensics is on it. They always are."

I explained to him what Uncle Darling told me about what the killer had said, and then I wondered out loud, "Do you think this a robbery gone bad? Did the killer have his own gun? I mean, did he hold up the store not realizing Gable had a gun, too? And did he steal anything from the register? And why didn't Gable push the silent alarm? Doesn't every convenience store have one?"

The questions came spilling out of my mouth, having built up while trying to keep my thoughts contained with Uncle Darling.

"I don't know about the alarm. I mean, I'm sure Mr. Feeney has one, but I can't figure why Gable didn't press it. Maybe he thought he could handle the guy because he had the shotgun? But the killer also didn't take a single thing," Stiles responded. "The register was never touched. No money missing, and Mr. Feeney said it didn't seem like any items were missing, either."

Still... "That still doesn't explain the SD card. Why would he want it if he was in disguise? I can't help but feel like there was something more on it than just him doing whatever he was doing in the store. Or am I conclusion-jumping here?"

"I guess it's possible, Kitten, but every criminal knows a store has a surveillance camera. Maybe he was just making sure no one ever saw it and there'd be no trace of him unless Monty could identify him. And how would he do that if he was wearing a ski mask?"

"But," I whispered into the dark of the barn, "he was fighting with Gable over the SD card. That's what Darling said. That happened for a reason. And something else that worries me sick, Monty probably did see him and hear whatever transpired between the killer and Gable. He's not safe, Stiles. That terrifies me."

"Ansel's already on it. He's going to post someone at the hospital as soon as Monty comes out of surgery. They'll keep him safe."

I blew out another anxious breath. "So I guess until Uncle Monty wakes up, we don't have much if the SD card is gone."

"Well, we don't have a lot, but we do have that

missing girl. They're sending Detective Godfrey out to talk to her parents tonight."

How awful for this poor girl's parents to know she was missing—and likely, the person who'd taken her had just tonight been in a convenience store but fifteen miles away.

But that lipstick… "What about that lipstick? If that girl's been missing for a few days, and the lipstick was only discovered tonight, the killer has to have some connection to her, right? He must have been the one who had it. I mean, Mr. Feeney probably cleans the bathrooms at minimum twice a day. No way would a lipstick be left lying around for as long as a couple of days. Especially in the *men's* bathroom. That makes me wonder if the missing girl wasn't on that SD card…"

"Good point. Except Mr. Feeney said he checks the video camera footage every two or three days, and he hasn't seen anything even a little suspicious, and he said he didn't recognize Kerry's photo at all. Besides that, Kerry couldn't have physically been in the store as of the last time he'd checked the footage two days ago."

Unless she was disguised when she came in? Or someone forced her to wear a disguise? Or was I just letting myself get carried away?

I plucked at my lip in nervousness, getting some fuzz from my gloves in my mouth. I had a lot to process and right now, I was so worried about Uncle Monty, I wasn't sure I was capable.

"Let's revisit this later. For right now, are you're sure it's okay to tell Hobbs?"

"Tell me what?"

I almost jumped out of my skin, whirling around to see the lights wrapped around the fence revealing Hobbs, his tall frame strutting through the doors of the barn with sure strides, his hands in the pockets of his favorite rawhide jacket.

I held up a finger to him to hear Stiles say, "How can you avoid it? Listen, Kitten. I think the time has come for you to consider telling Hobbs about your visions. You can't keep playing both sides of the fence and keep your sanity. Your visions have helped me a lot. They're not just about lost pieces of jewelry or hidden wills anymore. They're about real crimes, and seeing as you guys are thicker than thieves these days, he's going to start to wonder about your quote-unquote *migraines*."

I cast a sidelong glance at Hobbs, who was petting Nana's head and cooing at her. "How do you feel about the answer, I'll think about it?"

"I feel like you're avoiding the reality of this and it's going to bite you in the bum if you're not careful. You don't have to tell him you're a witch, Hal. Maybe for now that's too far, but he's no dummy."

"That's definitely too far," I whispered. The idea made my stomach jolt to life.

"And I get that, Kitten. But you can tell him you have visions. Look at it this way, he doesn't even have to believe you, because we both know you can prove him wrong. But he's sure gonna start to wonder how you're hip to so much sensitive information when I keep saying I can't confirm or deny any of the evidence you keep seeing. Not to mention, if he thinks I'm feeding you info, he's going to think I'm a shady cop. Either way, what's the worst he can say? You're full of stuffing and he walks away. That'll just mean he wasn't worth the time of day anyhow—even though I don't believe he's that kind of guy, right?"

Gulping, I nodded. "Right."

"I'm only telling you this because I love you. You know that, don't you?"

I hated when he hit me upside my head with a two by four of reason. "I do. Everything you're saying is true and I promise to give it some thought, okay?"

It was the only answer I could provide at this point. I had to know I could categorically, undeniably trust Hobbs. We'd only *really* known each other for a few months, and had only recently begun to spend much of our time together.

"Okay. I love you, Kitten. Kiss Uncle Darling for me."

He hung up the phone and I put mine in my back pocket, my hands cold, my thoughts swirling around in my head like leaves in an autumn windstorm.

Hobbs peered at me from Nana's stall, his eyes glittering. "Everything all right?"

"*Everything* is a subjective word. Listen, I have to tell —" My phone beeped, cutting me off. I held up my finger again and pulled my phone back out of my pocket to read a text from the hospital.

For the first time since I'd picked up Uncle Darling from Feeney's, I let out a cleansing breath.

"Uncle Monty's out of surgery and stable for now. So far, they haven't induced a coma, so the doctor said Uncle Darling can see him for a couple of minutes."

Hobbs let out a breath of air, too; it puffed into the interior of the cold barn. Then he smiled that wholesome cowboy grin. "Your car or mine?" he asked.

My heart lurched in my chest. Not only because Hobbs really comes across as a genuinely good guy, but because I liked him, and if I told him one of my secrets, and he rebuffed me, or worse, laughed at me and told me I was nuts, it was going to hurt.

A lot.

CHAPTER 6

The Little Drummer Boy
    Written by Katherine Kennicott Davis, Henry Onorati, Harry Simeone, 1941

*T*he ride as Hobbs drove us to the hospital in his Jeep was quiet. Uncle Darling lost in his thoughts but at least a bit calmer, and Hobbs concentrating on the road. I pondered not only what Stiles had said about telling Hobbs about my visions, but the missing girl, Kerry Carver.

I'd decided to relay the information Stiles gave me to Hobbs, sans my vision, and as we crossed the icy hospital parking lot, Uncle Darling clinging to Hobbs for dear life, I wasn't sure if I was glad I hadn't told him about my visions, or more stressed.

We walked into the lobby and headed for the elevators, still in silence, both of us holding on to Uncle Darling, who exhaled deeply.

When we stepped out the doors to the ICU unit, the sterile smell and the beep of life-saving machines couldn't be cheered with the Christmas decorations, though, they'd done their best. There was a small Christmas tree in the nurses' station reception area and silver garland hung from the front of the counter where the pleasant-looking nurse sat.

I approached with soft feet and smiled at the nurse behind the counter with glossy black hair and warm chocolate-colored eyes. "Hi there. I'm Hal Valentine—"

"Are you the lady who owns Just Claus?"

I smiled wider and held out my hand over the counter. "That's me. You are?"

She shook my hand with her dry, cool grip. "Belinda Espinoza. It's really nice to meet you. My aunt Rosalie works for you. Rosalie Lincoln?" Then she flapped her hands in a dismissive gesture. "You have a lot of people working for you. I'm sure you don't know who she is. How can I help you, Miss Valentine?"

I tapped the counter with my fingertip. "First, I do know Rosalie. She works in customer service, and all our customers ask for her because she's so bubbly and fun. She's also got at least a hundred pictures on hand of her grandchildren, Sophia and Max. We love her, and her laugh is infectious."

Her grin lit up her face. "That's Aunt Rosalie. No one escapes without seeing at least one picture of Sophia and Max. She'll be so thrilled to hear you remembered them because, according to her, there are no other grandchildren in the world. Now, my aunt's bragging aside, how can I help, Miss Valentine?"

"It's just Hal, and we're here to see my uncle, Montwell Danvers. Doctor Jordon said he's just out of surgery and Darl—er, his husband, Andrew Darkling, could see him for a few minutes. So we rushed right over. Can you help?"

She pulled a chart from the pile on the reception desk and nodded with another warm smile. "Yes. Of course. But only for a few minutes and only his husband, okay? You and your husband," she said, pointing to Hobbs, who had his arm around Uncle Darling's shoulders, "will have to wait outside."

My cheeks grew pink and my skin went hot. "He's not...um, my husband."

But Belinda wasn't paying any attention to me anymore. She came around the reception desk, her shoes padding softly along the white-tiled floor as she introduced herself to Uncle Darling and Hobbs.

Then she took his hand, and we trailed her as she led Darling into the ICU room, where the lights were dim and it felt like a thousand machines were lit up and monitoring Monty's life.

When I saw him there, for the briefest of moments, in that bed that looked as though it had swallowed him whole, hooked up to heart monitors and an IV drip, I choked up.

He looked so small, even though he was easily six feet, his face gaunt and slack under the effects of the anesthesia, his head bandaged in white gauze, his pale skin almost translucent under the dim light over his bed.

It was then I wished I could have gone in with Uncle Darling, who sobbed softly as Belinda led him to the bed.

When the door swung shut, I dropped my chin to my chest and squeezed my eyes closed. My throat grew tight, and I almost couldn't breathe from the fear I felt about the fact that we could lose Monty. I'd managed to keep it together for a few hours now for Uncle Darling's sake, but I didn't think I could keep doing that without a meltdown first.

Leaning forward, I braced my forehead on the wall and tried to force back my tears, but they wouldn't be thwarted. They rushed forward against my will, in all their hot saltiness, dropping to the white tile floor and leaving splotches of wet marks.

I adored Monty. Above all else, I adored that he adored my uncle. I loved that he'd convinced one very skeptical Andrew Darkling that love was real and if he'd just take a chance, he could spend the rest of his life reaping the benefits of passion, laughter and loyalty, but he had to allow Uncle Monty the chance to show him.

And he did take a chance, probably a bigger risk than he'd ever let on, and if the person who'd done this to my uncle got away with it, and took away what was most important to Darling, I'd hunt him for the rest of his miserable life.

And if I found him, I'd show him a thousand tortures with my magic, Atticus and the rules for mortals be hanged. I couldn't meddle with the cycle of life. I knew better than to use my magic to heal Uncle Monty, and so did Uncle Darling, but if he died because he was caught up in a robbery gone wrong and my uncle lost the one thing he cared about the most in this world?

Things would become very ugly.

As my anger and sorrow rose, Hobbs put his hand on my shoulder and gently turned me around, pulling me to his broad chest, and I let him.

I cried ugly, sloppy tears, jamming my fist to my mouth to keep from screaming out my anguish and frustration, and Hobbs didn't try to stop me.

He smoothed circles over my back as I wet his shirt with my muffled sobs and enjoyed the comfort of his broad chest and warm embrace.

I needed air. Lifting my head, I swiped my tears and looked up at Hobbs. "I need a minute. Can you wait here in case he's done before I get back?"

He cupped my chin and wiped my cheek with his thumb. "You bet. Text if you need me and I'll come running."

Turning, I hightailed it to the elevator and pressed the button, jumping in the second it arrived. I had to catch my breath and keep it together for Uncle Darling.

I jetted out into the lobby and made a break for the doors leading outside, letting the bitter cold hit my face and evaporate the tears on my cheeks.

Gulping the frosty air, I zipped up my jacket and tightened my scarf around my neck, looking out at the parking lot lights and gathering my senses. The ocean was a bit more distant from here, but I could still hear the crash of the occasional wave and smell the tangy salt, and I let it do what it did best—soothe me.

The parking lot was mostly deserted at this hour, giving me the added bonus of privacy.

"Miss Valentine," a voice from out of nowhere called.

I turned to find a neatly dressed man in a tweed coat, with cheerful eyes and a lean build, approaching me.

Wiping at my eyes, I acknowledged him. "That's me. What can I do for you?"

He held out a business card, his smile easy and warm. "My name is Abraham Weller, from Weller and Walgreen."

An attorney. Talk about gossip traveling fast in a small town. Instantly, my guard was up. "And?"

I made my aggravation clear in my tone, but that didn't deter him. "I hope you don't mind the intrusion, but I understand your uncle was involved in a murder this evening at Feeney's Fuel and Gruel?"

Perfect. Just what I needed. An ambulance chaser. Staring him directly in the eye, I glared. "I'm not at liberty to discuss anything. In other words, you're barking up the wrong tree, Mr. Weller. Go chase a different ambulance."

I'm not sure what made him back off, whether it

was my death glare or my direct words, but back off he did. "My apologies, but I hope you'll call on me if—"

"Goodnight, Mr. Weller," I said firmly, rather than punching him square in the nose with my clenched fist.

Thankfully, he took the hint and scurried off into the dark parking lot.

Unclenching my jaw, I forced back more tears of frustration and anger at how bold some folks were. My uncle was lying in a bed, his brain taken apart like a tinker toy and only just put back together again, and lugs like Weller were looking to score a lawsuit against Feeney's.

And make no mistake, that's what this was about. I'd almost bet he was interested in suing Feeney's for safety reasons or some such nonsense. Not only did Uncle Monty have more integrity than to hold Mr. Feeney responsible for an accident, so did my Uncle Darling.

Oh, I wanted to sock him in the nose!

As the doors of the lobby swished opened, in my haze of anger, I only vaguely saw two people come out and heard their whispers as they passed by. I was still pretty caught up in my own worries and fears when someone tapped me on the shoulder.

Turning, I was faced with Gable Norton's widow, Anna, a pretty blonde with bloodshot, swollen eyes, mussed clothes, and the appearance of the weight of the world on her shoulders.

She was with a woman who looked just like her but older, or maybe it was the other way around.

Instantly, I wanted to give her my condolences and offer my help, but she spoke before I had the chance. "You're Halliday Valentine, right?"

"I am, and you're Anna, right?"

"Ye...yes. And this is my mother, Regina," she said, pointing to the woman next to her.

Scanning her body and face, rigid with anguish, and wondering why she was at the hospital, I asked, "Are you all right? Are you hurt?"

She shook her head, her tangled hair sticking to her wet cheeks. "They made me come here to be sure I was okay. That's all. I'm fine. Fine."

I'd heard those words before. I'm fine, in Anna's case, meant she was barely holding it together. I hated that for her...for her newly born daughter...for Gable.

Regina shook her head firmly, pulling her red wool trench coat tighter around her chin. "She's not fine, Miss Valentine. She's a wreck. They had to give her a sedative to calm her down, she was so hysterical. That's why she's here."

"Mom, please!" Anna hissed, stomping her foot. "Be quiet and let me talk!"

I didn't want things to escalate, so I asked in as soothing a tone as possible, "What can I do for you, Anna? How can I help?"

"I..." She gasped, her shoulders jerking from the effort as she pulled her puffy jacket back up over her shoulders. "I need...I need to talk to you. *Please*."

Tears began to fill her red-rimmed eyes again, and that was when I took her hand. "How about we do it inside, okay? It's too cold for you to be out here." Tugging her hand, I led her back into the lobby and brought her to the row of dark brown chairs next to a table of magazines. "Tell me what I can do for you, Anna?"

"Gable," she hacked out, her chest heaving. "I need to ask you about Gable."

That took me a bit by surprise as I encouraged her to sit and looked into her tortured blue eyes. "Me? I'm not sure I understand."

She grabbed my hand and held it tight, as though she were clinging for her life. "You're the niece of the other man who was hurt at Feeney's, right?"

"I am," I offered quietly.

"Anna," her mother said with a softer tone, putting her hand on her daughter's shoulder and squeezing. "Maybe now's not the time, honey. She's in distress, too."

But she pushed her mother away and looked to me with broken eyes. "No, Mom, I have to know. I need to know what happened!" she cried, her hysteria clearly rising.

"What do you need to know?" I used great caution when I asked.

"Did your uncle tell you anything about what the man who killed Gable said? Did he say anything about...about *drugs*?"

I blinked in surprise, gripping her hand. "Drugs? Is that what the man was doing in Feeney's?"

"I don't know!" she wailed with a phlegm-filled

cough. "I don't know why he killed Gable. I don't understand!"

Turning to fully face her, I looked at her distraught face and held her hand tight. "I don't know what happened, Anna. My uncle's just out of a surgery about an hour ago, and his husband—we call him Uncle Darling—doesn't know either. He just walked in on—"

"The murder!" Anna shouted. "Gable was murdered in cold blood, and I want to know why! I need to know what happened to my husband. Everything was going really great. He was attending his meetings and he was sober. But he came home two nights ago and something was wrong. I *know* something was wrong!"

"Anna! You have to calm down, honey. This isn't good for you," her mother pleaded as people traipsing through the lobby began to stare.

But Anna yanked her arm away from her mother again. "No. *No,* Mother, I will *not* calm down. I know her uncle knows something. I know he had to have seen or heard *something*!"

"He's still heavily sedated, and he was unconscious when he was taken by ambulance from the scene. He only just came out of surgery, Anna. I can't help you until he wakes up, but do you mind if I ask you a question? What makes you think it was about drugs if Gable was sober?"

Her full lips thinned and her eyes went stormy. "Because he wasn't right when he came home from work, and he didn't smell like alcohol. When he was drinking, he always smelled like whiskey. I'd bet anything he was mixed up with that scuzzbucket Landry again. I'd bet my soul on it!"

I looked to her mother for help. "Who's Landry?"

Regina grimaced, her heart-shaped face, so like her daughter's, contorting. "He's who Gable used to hang out with when he was using, and for a while, he," she leaned down and whispered, "sold drugs for him."

I'd had no idea Gable was a drug user, too. I'd thought only alcohol was involved. And that name, Landry...I was sure I knew it.

Looking to Regina, I asked, "Wait, do you mean Landry Tithers? The one who used to play football at Marshmallow Hollow High?"

Regina made a face of sheer disgust. "That's the dirtball. I don't care what all of Gable's AA buddies say, Landry was the one who got him addicted, and if I get my hands on him, I'm going to kill him!"

Just then, Hobbs popped out of the elevator, his eyes concerned when they met mine as he crossed the room to where I was sitting with Anna.

"So you think Gable was mixed up in selling drugs again, and he was killed for it?"

"I don't know!" she cried, twisting her fingers together. "I don't know what's happening. Nothing is right anymore. He wouldn't talk to me, even though I knew something was wrong. But now he's dead. He's *dead* and our daughter's going to grow up without a father! I'll be alone forever! He wasn't supposed to leave us alone like this!"

Her hysteria left me feeling deeply anxious. I

couldn't imagine how torn up inside Anna must feel, and I hated that she was in such obvious agony. So I did the only thing I could think to do. I made her focus on me and tried to cast a quietly covert incantation.

"Anna, look at me, please," I urged as I tried to subtly create a calming spell. "Listen to my words. I heard this once somewhere, and while I don't remember who I heard it from, I hope it helps you. Will you listen?"

She nodded wordlessly when I took her hand, making circles on her palm, and whispered, "Soothe my soul in times of sorrow, give me peace until the morrow. Allow me these next hours' rest, for then I shall be ready for the test."

Anna stared at me for a moment...and then she relaxed, almost slumping against me.

Looking to Regina, whose blue eyes had gone wide, I gave her a sympathetic smile. "I think the meds have finally kicked in. Maybe now's the time to take her home? But please, take my number, and if you need anything or if Anna remembers anything else I can pass on or help with, she can call me. Day or night." I took her phone and typed in my number.

Regina gave me a grateful if not weary smile, tucking her bobbed hair behind her ears before scooping Anna up. "You've been very nice, Miss Valentine. Thank you for indulging her."

"It's nothing. Bundle up now, it's mighty cold out there," I reminded her before she helped Anna out of the lobby, and I turned to Hobbs. "Everything okay?"

He was staring at me so hard, his dark chocolate eyes so intense, I felt naked. But then he appeared to shake it off. "It depends on how you define okay. But first, let's talk about what just happened."

As I began to rise, I froze. "Talk about it?" I asked with a mouth as dry as the desert.

"Yeah! Holy smokes, Hal. You were really great with her. I'd like to know where you heard that quote, because it did the trick. I'm gonna look it up when we go home."

Oh, jeepers. Would I never learn? "And second?"

He sighed, his big chest rising and falling, his eyes unable to hide his concern. "Monty is awake."

I hopped all the way up and straightened, my heart pounding. "That's great, right?"

Hobbs stared at me again, but this time he put his hand on my arm. "Sort of."

I cocked my head and narrowed my eyes. "Explain?" I asked with a hesitant wince.

"He doesn't remember Uncle Darling."

Aw, come on, Universe. Cut it out!

CHAPTER 7

Last Christmas
  Written by George Michael, 1984

---

*W*e stood outside my uncle's ICU room and hovered there, unsure what to do. From the small window in the door, I saw my Uncle Darling struggle with the fact that Uncle Monty didn't appear to know who he was as he held his hand and kissed him goodnight.

Dr. Jordan had been very clear when he'd said Monty was still under the effects of the heavy anesthesia from a major surgery, and the loss of memory wasn't uncommon, but it had clearly shredded my uncle.

That blank stare—and even a bit of fear—in

Monty's eyes before he'd fallen back to sleep had shredded me, too.

As Belinda went in to collect Uncle Darling, I turned to Hobbs, knowing my eyes held the helplessness I was feeling.

He looked down at me, his expression filled with warmth and sympathy. "You heard the doctor, Hal. This could be only temporary. I know the inclination is to project, but for Uncle Darling's sake, try to avoid that."

"You're right. Logically, I hear you. Emotionally, I've gone deaf and can't hear anything but my uncle crying."

"Do you want the pep talk I have prepared?" he asked.

"You have pep talks all ready to roll out?"

"One for every occasion."

"Sure. Give it your best shot."

"We have a killer to catch, Hal. The only way we can do that and keep Monty from any possible further harm is to find the guy who did this."

The moment he said the words was the moment someone from Marshmallow Hollow PD showed up, tipping his hat to us as he placed a chair by Uncle Monty's door and sat down.

But Hobbs's words struck a chord in me and lit a fire in my belly. "You're right. Though, if there's an award for Best Detective of The Year, I'd like to remind you of our last," I swiped the air with my fingers, "investigation. We didn't exactly nail it."

Hobbs rolled his eyes at me. "Maybe Sherlock

Holmes isn't going to ask us to join his investigative club, but we did, in a very roundabout way, figure it out."

I fought a snort. "We fell into the answer. That's what we did, tripping and flubbing all the way."

"But we found the answer nonetheless."

"I like your go-get-'em attitude. But here's something to think about before you get involved, Hobbs. If he's worried my uncle saw something, and he thinks my *other* uncle might know something, too, he could come looking back at the house. It could get dangerous. So I want you to know you can back out at any time."

He lifted his bearded chin and shook his dark head. "Nope. This cowboy's in it for the long haul."

My body tingled from head to toe, and I had to fight off a fresh batch of tears. Instead of sobbing in gratitude, I offered him my fist to bump. "Then yeehaw, Lacey. Let's do this."

He mock sighed at me and rolled his eyes. "How quickly we forget. *I'm* Cagney with the good hair, remember?"

I managed a tiny giggle. "Right, right. I'm Lacey with the mediocre coif."

Uncle Darling came out of Monty's room then, looking ragged and defeated, his shoulders slumped, his coat dragging beside him. He walked straight into the arms I held out to him. When he collapsed against me for the second time today, I hugged him close.

Taking his hand, I led him away the way he'd done

75

with me when I'd scraped my knee or my heart had been broken by some silly boy. "Let's get you home, Uncle Darling. We'll let Uncle Monty get some rest, and I bet things will look better tomorrow."

Uncle Darling didn't say a word as I helped him put his coat back on and wrapped his scarf around his neck, pressing a quick kiss to his chubby cheek.

Neither Hobbs nor I spoke, either, as we filed back into the elevator, and it remained that way while Hobbs heated up his Jeep and we waited in the lobby for him to come get us, then continued on the ride home.

Fighting my desolation and fears to stay strong for my uncle, I focused on Hobbs's words about finding the killer.

I wanted to find whoever did this and zap them to kingdom come. For Anna and Gable and their new baby.

For my uncles Monty and Darling.

"Is he resting comfortably?" Hobbs asked when I entered the kitchen.

He sat at my walnut-stained dining room table, his head poking out from behind a miniature sleigh filled with candy canes and greens.

He held up a cup of hot chocolate and enticed me to sit with him.

I took a chair at the table across from him and

smiled, taking the mug to find some of the fresh, homemade marshmallows I'd brought home bobbing in the chocolatey goodness.

"He is. He took a bit of a sleeping aid to help him get some rest. I think for the moment, he'll be okay."

By the way, in witch-speak, that means I cast a spell on him to keep him asleep and dreamless for the next eight hours or so.

"Good. He's had a hellish night," Hobbs said, pushing his phone at me. "So, I've been doing some digging around about Gable Norton, his wife Anna, and that missing girl you told me about, Kerry Carver."

I looked down at his phone as I took a sip of my hot chocolate, and my eyes widened. "Wait, am I reading that right? There are two more missing girls?" As I quickly scanned the article by a guy named Westcott Morgan, I almost gasped.

Hobbs drummed his fingers on the table, his lips a thin line under his neatly trimmed mustache. "That's correct. This guy Westcott wrote an opinion piece on the police department's lack of interest after talking to Jasmine Franks's mother. I guess Jasmine's mom thinks they dropped the ball, because they did next to nothing about Jasmine's disappearance other than to make her feel as though her daughter was off on some adventure. And because both she and the other girl, Lisa Simons, are basically adults, there's been very little done."

"So their disappearances aren't suspect because they're legal adults and maybe they ran off with some guy, that type of thing?"

"Yep. When Lisa went missing, they also did nothing. He has a theory about these girls and their economic backgrounds. He thinks their abductions are all connected. I mean, look at their pictures. All brunettes, average height, every one of them has blue eyes, all within the same age range. Makes sense, right? But his assertation is Jasmine and Lisa have a different socioeconomic background than Kerry, and maybe that's why no one's been making a fuss. He's calling it class discrimination."

"So Kerry's parents are making a stink and the Chester Bay police are taking note? Or is the truth just that she's underage and they'd look stupid to chalk it up to running off with a boyfriend?"

Hobbs's lips thinned. "It looks like they're at least looking into it a little harder than they did the other two girls. Not by much mind you. Basically, what Westcott's doing is stirring up controversy by heavily suggesting Jasmine and Lisa weren't worthy of the police's time because of their socioeconomic status. That's his angle, anyway. He doesn't really have a lot of facts to back it up, because let's face it, Kerry's disappearance is brand new and she's underage, but he's getting noticed, which is typically a journalist's hope— even if he's going about it salaciously."

Blinking, I set my mug down and went to get my laptop so I could see these girls clearer. Popping it open, I typed in the article and pulled it up, making the pictures of the young girls bigger.

Staring at their pretty faces, so young and dewy soft, my stomach turned and my hands went clammy.

I bit the tip of my fingernail, feeling a headache forming as I finished reading the article. "So this guy Westcott seems to be talking possible serial killer without saying serial killer, or at least that's what this article feels like he's implying. He makes some good points, too. Add to the similarities in their looks, age, etcetera, he says there's something else to consider— they're all from nearby towns."

Hobbs bobbed his head. "Uh-huh. All within a thirty or forty-mile radius, all very similar in looks, all ranging in age from seventeen to twenty, all missing within the last few months, with Kerry Carver being the most recent at three days ago."

"All traveling on foot." Cracking my knuckles, I rolled my head from side to side and remembered we hadn't discussed what Anna told me. "Before we get sidetracked on this, let me bring you up to speed with what I learned from Gable's wife, and her mother, Regina."

Hobbs held up his finger and nodded. "Before you show me yours, let me show you mine. While you were tucking in Uncle Darling, I also looked up Gable. He's had a handful of DUIs, a drunk and disorderly, and a couple of arrests for disturbing the peace. And I found on the Facebook page of a friend of a friend of Anna's that his rehab was court ordered."

"But no drug charges?"

"Nope. Not listed online, anyway. But everything's

online these days, so I don't know how it could have been missed. Mostly the devil he knew was booze. Also, nothing out of the ordinary on his own Facebook page but a lot of bad grammar and memes about hunting and football."

His comment made me snicker. "Bad grammar? Are you one of those people, Hobbs?"

He smirked at me, his eyes amused. "I told you, I do a lot of crossword puzzles. I like a solid vocabulary and good spelling. So I guess I am one of *those people*, and I'm not going to apologize for it. Anyway, why would you mention drugs in connection with Gable?"

I passed on what Regina had told me about Landry Tithers. "The fact that Anna wondered about whether Gable was selling again for Landry makes *me* wonder if he just never got caught with drugs. She said he'd been weird for a couple of days, but he didn't smell like alcohol. She assumed his strange behavior had to do with drugs."

Hobbs stretched his long arms out in front of him. "Then possible scenario? Landry Tithers maybe sold him drugs, or tried to get Gable to sell drugs *for* him, and he was the guy who shot Gable?"

"That's definitely a possibility, I suppose. Let's look up Landry and see what kind of charges, if any, he's got."

I don't know Landry Tithers personally. I only knew of him, and what I knew wasn't good.

"Already done," Hobbs said, showing me the screen

of his phone. "A couple of possession charges, one possession with the intent to sell."

"But nothing violent?"

"No assault. Though he does have one resisting arrest. I guess that could be considered violent, depending on how you define it, but no real history of violence. Just a bunch of drug charges."

"Then there's the SD card, the one Uncle Darling heard the killer talking about, what does that mean?" I put my head in my hands and groaned. "I can't make any sense of why the killer would want that if he was disguised by a mask. According to Uncle Darling, the killer said, and I quote, 'Give me that effin' SD card' like he specifically came to the store for it, as proven by the fact that he didn't steal anything, according to Stiles, and no merchandise was missing. Was the SD card the reason he was in the store in the first place?"

He cupped his chin. "I don't think it's such a stretch to think a criminal wouldn't want to be on any tape, even disguised, but I think you're right. I *think*. I don't think it has as much to do with recognizing him and more to do with something he did. But then that begs the question, what's on the SD card that's so bad he was willing to kill for it? And if it's Landry Tithers, is he the kind of guy who'd wear pants with a crease down the front? Because look at this picture of him. He's unshaven and a little scraggly. Does he look like the kind of guy who wears pants with a crease—a big enough crease for fashion-forward Uncle Darling to notice?"

As I stared at the picture of Landry Tithers, I definitely questioned whether he was a candidate for murder, considering what Uncle Darling told us. He was indeed unkempt and greasy and even a bit scrawny. I don't know that he could have wrestled a gun from Gable without help.

"And here's something else to think about," Hobbs said. "Maybe the SD card isn't from Feeney's at all? Maybe, whoever killed Gable wanted an SD card that had nothing to do with Feeney's at all. Maybe that just happened to be where he confronted him about it? Maybe the card is from a phone or a camera?"

Now my head was spinning. "I say we move on from our only suspect at this point and look up the missing girls' Facebook pages and Twitter handles, maybe see if we can dredge up any clues from them. I don't understand the connection between Kerry Carver's lipstick, the murderer, and Gable Norton, but I think we should try and look for one."

"Sounds like a plan," Hobbs agreed.

As I stared at the pictures of the missing girls, I had to agree with Westcott. His theory didn't seem so outlandish. "I have to admit, I don't know about the economic angle of things, but the rest of it? Westcott might be on to something. Their looks coupled with how they were taken, all walking somewhere, it's all very similar. But can we call him a serial killer if no one has turned up dead? Is that why I haven't heard about it on the news? I mean, there are no bodies to speak of. Or that we know of. Just a lipstick."

Hobbs steepled his hands in front of his mouth. "Serial kidnapper? Is that even a thing? I don't know. The only thing I *do* know is, I think this guy Westcott has a point, and I wonder if there are more girls we don't know about."

A violent chill ran along my spine. "Maybe we should email him? See if he gets back to us? He might not want to talk to us, but it's worth a try."

Hobbs took his phone back. "I'll do it."

"When you're done, you take Jasmine Franks, who's been missing for two months, and look at her Face-book page. I'll take Kerry Carver and the other girl, Lisa Simons—who, by the way, has been missing for three months."

As we both took to the task of scouring Facebook pages and Twitter timelines, a comfortable silence fell between us, the clack of my fingers on my keyboard the only interruption.

When my eyes became gritty and sore, I looked away from the computer, reaching up toward the ceiling to stretch my arms. "I've got a big fat bupkiss from these Facebook and Twitter pages. How about you?"

Hobbs squeezed his temples and ran a hand through his thick, dark hair. "Same here. Other than the initial details of their alleged abductions, and the pleas for their safety and for the police to look into it, there's not much else. There are tons of prayers being sent up and 'I miss you's' posted, but nothing that sends up any smoke signals."

Looking at the time on my laptop, my hot chocolate long gone cold, I realized it was almost two in the morning, and that made me yawn. "I'm going to send the girls' parents a message on Facebook and see if they won't talk to me."

Hobbs reached across the table and laced his fingers with mine. "You're exhausted. You need to get some rest, Hal."

But not him. He looked fresh as a daisy. "How come you look like you just rolled out of bed after a refreshing twelve-hour nap?"

He shrugged and grinned sheepishly as he tucked his phone into his back pocket. "I'm a night owl, I guess. I'm used to being up this late."

"Oh, yeah, I remember seeing the lights on in the cottage one night when I got up for some aspirin. It was pretty late, as I recall."

"I like the night. We see eye to eye on a lot of things. The peace and quiet being one of them. No phones, no doorbells. It's a great time to do a crossword puzzle."

Chuckling, I understood. Running a busy factory, I spent the day with a lot of boisterous workers, not to mention some rather noisy machines. Peace and quiet was a small blessing from time to time.

"So let's call it a day for the moment? Uncle Darling's going to need all my attention tomorrow, with the way things are shaping up with Uncle Monty, but fingers crossed these girls' parents will at least give me the time of day."

Hobbs rose and grabbed his coat, pulling it over his

arms. "Okey-dokey. I'll do some more poking around online before I go to bed, but if you're okay with it, I'll be back tomorrow to help out."

My heart clenched in my chest. "That would be really nice. I'll make sure we have plenty of biscuits and gravy ready in your honor."

He grinned, his expression surprised. "You know how to make biscuits and gravy?"

I didn't, but I bet Atti did, and what good was magic if you couldn't use it to make someone else happy? At least, that was how I planned to sell it to Atti.

"Don't you worry your little cowboy head about what I know," I said in a really bad Southern accent. "Just be back here for breakfast around nine or so."

Making his way around the table, he grabbed my fingers and gave them a squeeze. "See you then, Hal. G'night."

He whistled to Stephen King, who'd been lying by the fireplace in the dining room, and the next thing I heard was the jingle of the door as it closed. Then, for the moment, I was alone.

Inhaling deeply, I closed my eyes and rubbed my temples.

"Headache, Poppet?" Atti asked, his deep voice resonating in my ear as he flew to my shoulder, his soft wings brushing against my forehead.

"Tension headache, I guess. Tension and worry about Uncle Monty and Uncle Darling. How are *you*?"

He brushed his wing along my cheek, his deep voice full of concern when he said, "Worried about you."

Tears stung my eyes again and my throat grew tight. "Don't worry, Atti. I'm going to find who did this to Uncle Monty and Gable Norton, and when I do…"

"Come, Poppet. I've turned down your bed and made a fire. Let's get your thermals on and tuck you in. The Sandman is calling your name. Tomorrow will bring with it new perspective."

I rose and followed Atti down the hall to my bedroom, feeling helpless and scared while, strangely, Phil loomed at my heels.

Now more than ever, I wished my mother Keeva was here to help me soothe Uncle Darling. What if Uncle Monty's memory loss wasn't only because of the anesthesia? What if he didn't remember the one person who loved him more than almost anything else?

If that was the case, my mother would know what to do. She'd know what to say.

Stripping off my clothes, I put on the thermal pajamas Atti had so kindly laid out at the end of my bed and climbed under the thick comforter. The fire roared in all its purple and orange glory, the Christmas lights on the mantel twinkled, and outside, the ocean crashed against the rocks.

Phil hopped up on the bed and brushed against me, rubbing his oddly shaped head on my cheek. Yes, the Phil who can barely contain his disdain for me was making actual physical contact.

I sniffled and reached for him, wrapping my arms around his neck—and he did what Phil does, he squirmed out of my reach and stared at me as though

I'd offended him with my needy desperation and my grabby hands.

"Too much, buddy?" I whispered, my throat tight.

He glared, his glassy green eyes sending one of his angry messages.

I smiled at him despite the ache in my heart. "That's what I thought."

But as I snuggled under the covers and Atti took his place beside me on his pillow, Phil did something very uncharacteristic. He snuggled up in the crook of my knees.

Maybe things weren't as helpless as they felt, after all.

CHAPTER 8

Do They Know it's Christmas?
Written by Bob Geldof and Midge Ure, 1984

I was feeling a little under the weather with a stuffy nose as I watched Hobbs push the last of his breakfast into his mouth before wiping it with a napkin.

"I gotta give it to you, Hal. For a Yankee, those were some dang good biscuits and sausage gravy. Real close to my mama's."

I blushed as I pushed mine around my plate. I couldn't take credit for making the meal. Atti's magic could.

We all sat around the dining room table in the cold morning light. The sun was out, glinting on the ocean outside the windows, but that wouldn't last for long if we listened to the forecaster from the morning news.

Snow was in the forecast for tonight, when Hobbs and I had a date for the Christmas tree lighting in the square. But this morning, we were going to find Landry Tithers, and early this afternoon, after getting an email from him in response to Hobbs, we were going to meet with Westcott Morgan.

"I'm glad you liked it. Uncle Darling?" I looked across the table at him, his eyes red and weary even after eight solid hours of sleep. "Won't you try and eat something for me? Please? I know your appetite is suffering, but you need your strength for today. Uncle Monty's awake, and that's amazing news."

I almost burst into more tears when I got the text from Belinda just as she was preparing to leave her night shift. Uncle Monty was awake again, and she said Dr. Jordon told her Darling could visit when visiting hours began at ten.

"I know you'll probably think this is crazy, Lamb, considering the size of the caboose on my choo-choo train, but I'm not a stress eater. No disrespect to your homage to the delicious cowboy and the great state of Texas. I'm just not very hungry," he said, his raspy voice low on energy.

Maybe my sleeping spell wasn't as great as I'd thought.

Hobbs's face turned bright red. "None taken, Uncle Darling. Can I get you more coffee?"

Uncle Darling smiled at him faintly, and ever so

coquettishly. "The only thing you can get me is another one of you."

I giggled because I was exhausted and glad to see a glimmer of the man I knew. "You are incorrigible," I chastised.

"I," he said with a saucy wiggle of his eyebrows, "am truthful. Better nab this one pronto before some other cowgirl comes along and lassos him right out from under your pert little nose!"

Now *my* face was the one turning red. "You hush and go get Monty's things together. I'm sure he'd love his toothbrush at this point."

Instantly, his shoulders sagged under his freshly pressed button-down shirt. "But will he remember what a toothbrush is? That's the million-dollar question."

Hobbs wrapped his arm around Uncle Darling's shoulders and gave him a pat on his arm. "If not, we'll remind him, because my mama always said good oral hygiene is important."

Uncle Darling reached up and pinched his cheek before brushing his knuckles over it. "You're not just pretty to look at, are you, sweet boy?" He pressed a kiss to Hobbs's fingers and was off to gather Uncle Monty's things to take to the hospital as I collected the plates from the table.

I was busy going through the events of last night when I remembered I had a loose end—that ambulance chaser, Abraham Weller, whose card was still in my jacket pocket.

"Just a head's up. A guy by the name of Abraham Weller tried a bid at ambulance chasing with me last night at the hospital, about Uncle Monty. Be on the lookout for shady lawyers in tweed jackets. I don't want anyone scaring Monty any more than he already is."

He pointed to his eyes. "I'll keep 'em wide open. Anything from the missing girls' parents?"

"Not a single thing. They probably think I'm another reporter. I'm sure after that Westcott's article, where he insinuates Kerry Carver's parents are getting all the police love, no one's going to want to talk to me. But I'll try to find an address for them, and maybe we can pay them a visit."

Fighting a yawn, I dropped the plates in the sink and planned to rinse them, but Hobbs beat me to it. "You made breakfast, I'll clean up," he said with an affable smile.

Oh, Hobbs, if you only knew how breakfast got on the table.

"Did you get any sleep last night, Cagney with the good hair?" I asked as I wiped down the counters and avoided staring at his broad back.

He popped open my stainless-steel dishwasher and began dropping dishes into it. "I did, Lacey, but not before I spent a good hour internet surfing for more stuff on the three missing girls, Gable and Landry Tithers."

Stephen King came snorting his way over to me, and I scooped his chunky body into my arms, giving him a hug and a kiss on the top of his head. "Did you find anything of interest or more of what we already found?"

"Not a lot of interest. Though, I did look at Anna's page and found an interesting comment from a Patricia Fowler."

"Interesting how?" I asked as I pulled a dog biscuit I'd bought especially for Stephen King out of a tin decorated in gingerbread men and showed it to Hobbs for permission.

He smiled and nodded before clearing his throat. "Well, the best I can figure from the conversation is, Patricia's son, Evan Fowler—was also an addict—often spent his time with Gable and Landry. Unfortunately, Evan died of a suspected overdose...and Patricia blames Gable."

I gave Stephen King his biscuit and one last kiss on the top of his head before setting him in front of the roaring fireplace, in the dog bed I'd also purchased just for him.

I pulled my phone from my pocket and hooked up to Anna's page. I saw the thread on Gable's death and began reading. "She blames Gable for her son's death?"

Hobbs wiped his hand on the red Christmas tea towel, closed the dishwasher and nodded. "Yep. Read her comment under all the condolences people were posting. I don't know if it's still there. Maybe Anna deleted it, but if so, I saved a screenshot."

It was easy enough to locate, and when I read her comment, my eyes widened. "Holy—"

Atticus, the foul language police, came buzzing directly at my head, preventing me from swearing.

"Spit. Holy, holy spit."

"Yeah," Hobbs drawled. "It's pretty bad."

As I read what Patricia wrote, I saw between the lines a mother who'd lost her child to an insidious disease, and it broke my heart.

Your good-for-nothing husband and that Landry Tithers killed my Evan and then left him to die! He has blood on his hands, Anna Norton, and he deserved to die for his sins! Gable Norton is a murderer, and don't you forget it!

"That's worse than I could have ever imagined." I leaned against the counter where Hobbs was rinsing out the sink. "Do you think we should add Patricia Fowler to our suspect list? Uncle Darling is still convinced it was a man who killed Gable, but a woman is possible, right?"

Hobbs folded the towel and grimaced. "It feels like a stretch, but stranger things have happened, right? We don't have a lot to go on, so I guess it couldn't hurt to add her to the pool."

"While Uncle Darling visits with Monty, I'd like to ask around about Gable and see if we can hook up with Landry."

"You do realize I'm not lettin' you talk to a drug dealer alone, right?"

My brow furrowed and my lips popped in aggravation. "I don't need a man to—"

"I don't care what you say you don't need. I'm twice as big as you and likely three times as strong. Those are just stats, Hal. Facts, if you will. No way I'm letting you look for a killer in a drug den alone. And I'm not going to hear a word about it."

"I have to agree with the strapping cowboy, Lamb. I don't want you chatting up drug lords without protection, and this hunky-hunk is the man to provide some," Uncle Darling said, reentering the kitchen.

But I wasn't hearing him—the world had stopped all motion and my heart took to skipping beats as it slowed.

I was in Feeney's again, peering into the men's bathroom like some voyeur. They were by the old, rusty sink Mr. Feeney was always talking about replacing but hadn't since as far back as I could remember.

Gable was fighting with the killer, Uncle Monty was on the floor under the towel dispenser, bleeding everywhere.

The toilet seat had spatters of blood on it, and it dripped down the side to pool on the floor.

Goddess, there was so much blood... The shot rang out again, and Gable dropped to the floor, broken and pale, looking as though a bomb had gone off in his chest. I saw the lipstick on the floor with no cap on it, its pink color glistening under the harsh lights of the bathroom.

And then everything slowed down, slowed so much it sounded like a Charlie Brown special when the adults speak in the background. That was when the most curious thing of all happened.

A typewriter appeared out of thin air, sitting right

on the sink, sticking out like a sore thumb. It was one of the old ones, a manual typewriter, if I'm not mistaken.

Black and shiny, the keys sank and rose as though someone's fingertips were actually hitting them, and then I heard a distinct ding, as if an invisible hand hit the carriage and carried over to the next line.

And then, like some sick slow-motion replay, the killer and Gable were struggling again. Yet, I reached out to try to touch the typewriter in the midst of Gable and the killer fighting over the gun, I don't know why, or what inspired me to try. I could never move when I had a vision, and I knew that even while in the height of one.

As usual, I was left frozen in place, but I tried to reach for it anyway, my limbs feeling like thick, heavy sausages.

Suddenly, a scent reached my nose, one I distinctly knew because of my ex-fiancé.

Smoke.

Someone smelled like cigarette smoke.

I'd know that smell anywhere. Hugo was a some-time smoker, and he often had the lingering scent on his suit jackets or in his hair.

How odd. I couldn't remember ever having a scent-o-vision… Technicolor? Yes. A scent? No.

I came back to the land of the living with my Uncle Darling on one side of me and Hobbs on the other. Atti was on my shoulder, rubbing his head against my cheek.

"There she is. There's my Lamb," I heard Uncle Darling coo in my ear as he brushed the hair from my face. "Another one. Isn't that two in two days, Lovey?"

As the haze of my vision cleared, I tried to parse his words, but could only nod.

"Do you want something to drink? An aspirin?" Hobbs asked, holding my hand with loose fingers.

"No," I whispered. Then I stood up straight and cleared my throat. "No. I'm all right."

Hobbs smiled down at me, the deep grooves on either side of his mouth so appealing. "Boy, those are humdinger migraines, huh? Maybe it's all the stress of the past couple of days? Maybe you should stay in and rest today?"

But I shook my head and blew out a breath. "It's passed now, Hobbs. How about we get you to the hospital so you can spend some time with Uncle Monty, Darling? The doctor said you can't stay long, but I bet he can't wait to see you."

"Oh-oh-oooh!" he poo-pooed with a squeak, fanning himself in dramatic Uncle Darling fashion. "That's if he remembers me at all."

"Well, we won't know until we go find out. Am I right? Grab your coat and I'll get my things and we'll do this together. Remember what Mom used to say?" I asked as I headed toward the mudroom with him in tow.

"You can't face your fears if you're hiding under the covers," he answered.

I jabbed a finger in the air. "Exactly. So pull those covers off and let's get this chuckwagon rollin'."

But Uncle Darling grabbed me and squeezed my arm while Hobbs went to the front door to get his coat. "Speaking of chuckwagons, Cowboy's a keeper, Lambykins. A real keeper. Uncle Darling approves."

Rolling my eyes, I made a face at him, even if his approval warmed my soul. "Why, because he wants to protect me from the big bad drug dealer? I think you know I can handle myself, Uncle Darling."

"No. Because you should have seen the look on his face when you had your," he cleared his throat, "migraine. That was genuine concern on his chiseled face, honey. Gen-u-wine. Also, I like him. I'm not mad at how good-looking he is to rest my old eyes upon, either."

Sighing, I grabbed my coat and hat as Uncle Darling followed behind. "Things have been really hectic here, Darling. Now's not the time to make life decisions."

He stopped me then and bracketed my face with his warm hands. "There's always time for love, Lamb."

"Love? We only really started to get to know one another each other not long ago. I'm not in—"

"Fiddlesticks, Lamb. When the thunderbolt strikes, it strikes. Time matters not. I'm not saying you should set a date and go wedding-cake tasting yet. I'm only saying, don't miss out. Leave room in your life for some romance. Your mother would kill me if I didn't tell you that. It's worth it." Then he gave me an impish Uncle Darling grin. "Well, unless he gets whacked on the head and can't remember who his husband is. Then it's not such a scream." He dropped a kiss on my nose and smiled genuinely, for the first time since he'd arrived. Smiled like the old Uncle Darling once had. "So promise your uncle you'll at least think about it."

Oh, I thought about it all the time. If he only knew how much I thought about it. But I didn't tell him that. I wasn't ready to show my cards yet. My deck was stacked, and I had a hand full of royal flushes.

Squeezing his hand, I nodded. "Promise."

"Good girl. Now, let me go find our hunk." He went off in the direction of Hobbs, leaving me to get the rest of my stuff together and say goodbye to my much-neglected familiar.

Taking Atti off my shoulder, I set him on my finger and I kissed his head. "You behave while I'm gone. Stay away from Phil. He looked especially longingly at you with those hungry eyes of his this morning. I promise we'll try and catch up tonight. I love you, Atticus Finch."

He buzzed in front of my face to let me know he heard me before darting off through the kitchen and down the hall.

I found Uncle Darling waiting by the front door. "Where's Hobbs?" I took a quick glance at my hair in the mirror in the entryway, smoothing it with my hands before pulling on my favorite oatmeal-colored hat.

"Warming up his Jeep for us." He clucked his tongue at me. "Like I said, he's a keeper. Now, before we go, do you want to tell me what that vision was about? I'm so caught up in me, I forget how selfish I'm being."

"It was pretty much the same as the last one, only this time it had, of all things, a typewriter in it."

"Now if that ain't whistling Dixie, I don't know what is," he remarked. "Oh, by the way, just before you put that spell on me last night—and don't think I don't know what a sleeping spell feels like, Miss Witch—I remembered something about the store. But I was too tired to move my big mouth."

I froze at the mirror where I was still fiddling with my hair and wondering if I shouldn't have some auburn streaks added to lighten up the coal black. "What did you remember?"

"You know how sensitive my nose is, right? I can smell what brand of fabric softener someone uses on their clothes from a country mile away."

Uncle Darling definitely had a touchy olfactory. "I do remember."

"And remember that one time when you thought you were a smart girl and would give smoking a try? Not even a shower could get rid of the smell?"

I did remember that. He'd smelled it on my jacket after I'd showered. His nose was uncanny. "Yup. I remember that, too."

"Well, get this, Lamb. I remembered smelling smoke at Feeney's. When that horrible man ran past me, he stunk of cigarette smoke."

Dum-da-dum-dum-duuuum...

CHAPTER 9

My Favorite Things
   Written by Oscar Hammerstein II, Richard
Rodgers, 1959

"This hardly looks like somewhere a drug dealer would hang out, Hal."

We were parked outside of Dessert Storm, the local bakery in town, owned by proud veteran Rhonda Jackson.

Rhonda had a wide smile, a warm hug, and apparently, according to some of the kids who took karate classes, a hiza geri (that's a knee strike, for all you laymen like me) that was deadly.

She'd recently retired from the Army and had come home to Marshmallow Hollow to open a bakery, finally fulfilling her secret pastry chef passions.

And I'm here to testify, her red velvet cupcakes with butterscotch frosting are like moist bites of Shangri-La made with the hands of anointed angels. Just ask me and the three I'd had only the other day for lunch.

I hadn't told Hobbs what my Uncle Darling had said about smelling smoke, but it was really bugging me. We'd both smelled it, but was my vision reliable and was Uncle Darling's memory correct?

I mean, it had sounded pretty scary. Out of all the things to remember, who'd remember something like smelling smoke when you were faced with a guy with a shotgun? But then, he'd remembered the crease in the killer's pants. I guess it wasn't that unusual.

Anyway, in other news, we'd decided to ask Landry some questions while my uncle visited with Monty, to keep my mind busy.

I peered at the gorgeous interior of the store with its beautiful chandelier lights and pinkish rose-gold walls and furniture. Rhonda had modeled it after one she'd been to when she was stationed in France, and it was every little girl's dream—filled with confections galore in pastel colors.

I made a face at him. "This is where Landry works, Hobbs. Look at his Facebook page. That's what it says."

Hobbs rolled his tongue along the inside of his cheek. "I can't believe a drug dealer works someplace so…so pink."

"Rhonda's known not just for her incredible baking skills and karate moves, she's also known for her big heart. Like Mr. Feeney, she does a lot of volunteer work at the church and the rec center. I'd almost bet she hired him at Mr. Feeney's request. Now let's get a move-on and see what we can see."

As we hopped out of the car and headed toward Rhonda's, I smiled at how beautiful it looked with its pink-and-white striped awning over the picture window and the soft pink of the brick façade she'd managed to talk the town council into letting her paint.

Oyster-white columns flanked a door etched in gold lettering with the bakery's very appropriate name for a woman who was proud to have served her country. Two cone-shaped topiaries in white vases sat on either side, with white twinkling lights on them.

We stopped at the entrance and I pointed inside. "Now, listen to me. I know how you feel about a good pastry. Or most sweets in general. But, and I can't stress this enough, don't let the luscious aroma of croissants and other delicacies deter you from the mission."

He saluted me. "Right. Question Landry Tithers about where he was last night and why Patricia Fowler thinks he's partially responsible for her son's death. Let no cupcake made from the tears of a saint put asunder."

I smirked and jabbed my finger in the air. "Exactly. And I'm here to tell you, it won't be easy to fight off the scent of frosting and freshly baked petit fours, but you must stay on task."

I might not have known Hobbs for long, but I knew his appetite for sweets could be insatiable. He loved cookies and cake, and he especially loved chocolate, but Twizzlers were his one true love.

He pulled the door open with a grin. "Swear it on my bag of chocolate Twizzlers. After you, Cowpoke."

Slipping inside, I sighed at the incredible smells and the pink tinted glass cases, filled with rows upon rows of pastel-colored treats.

The enormous chandelier hung over us, positioned at the center of the raised-tray ceiling in white. Smaller recessed lighting dotted the ceiling above cases, making everything sparkle and glow.

There were pink and white ornaments strung everywhere, a small white Christmas tree in the corner and string after string of twinkling lights, floating end to end in the space. Christmas music in French, seeping into the air, completed the whole feel of the store—giving it what Rhonda had explained she hoped would be an "experience."

"Ooohh," Hobbs murmured, his eyes wide.

I tugged on the arm of his jacket. "Hey. Stop being bedazzled and stick to the mission."

"Hal? Girl, is that you?"

I turned to see one of my favorite shop owners on the planet. Not only because she had amazing baked goods, but because she was so kind and friendly. She almost always had a good word about everyone, and if you were having a bad day, Rhonda somehow sensed it and offered a confection of consolation on the house.

She'd come from the back where the kitchen was located, her raven hair under her pastry chef's hat, her pleasantly round, solid body covered in a double-breasted white jacket with gold and pink buttons.

Rhonda held out her arms to me, her coal-black eyes twinkling, and I went straight into them, letting her hug me hard. "How are you, my friend? You look great and the store looks amazing!"

She dropped a kiss on my cheek. "Well, the store looks amazing because you helped me design it, kiddo."

Hobbs twirled his finger around. "You did…this?"

She swatted a tea towel in the air. "Yeah, she did. If not for Hal, this would be some tables and a chair and a lot of cake. I showed her what I'd seen in France, and she made it happen with her interior design contacts. And voila!"

I grinned at her, so pleased she was happy with her life and the dream she'd worked so hard to achieve. "It was your vision, my friend. I just drew a picture of what you wanted."

"Oh, petunias," she scoffed with a smile. "This happened because of you and I won't hear any different. Now, what can I do for you today, pretty lady, and who's this fine-lookin' fella?"

Hobbs put his hand out to Rhonda. "Hobbs Dainty, ma'am. Pleasure to meet you. I rent the cottage behind Hal's. I'm new around these parts."

Her eyes went wide and her smile wider as she pushed her hands into the wide pockets of her jacket. "Do I detect a bit of a Southern accent? Where from?"

He grinned. "Texas."

She rocked back on her heels. "Uh-huh. A Southern

boy. Had a sergeant from Texas. Dallas, I think it was. Fine man to have served with."

Hobbs grinned wider. "Yes, ma'am. A fine place indeed."

I decided to get right to the heart of the matter. "Listen, Rhonda, I'm here to ask you a couple of questions about an employee of yours. I'm guessing you heard about Gable Norton's murder last night?"

She clucked her tongue before she blew out a breath. "I sure did. Cryin' shame is what that is. I sent over some croissants to that poor child Anna and her mother this morning. At least they'll have a little something to put in their bellies, but Greer said they looked pretty torn up." She shook her head then, her eyes two deep pools of sorrow. "I thought he'd really gotten himself together, but now the rumor mill's talkin' about drugs and whatnot. Smells fishy."

Greer was Rhonda's life partner, and her partner in Dessert Storm, and equally as warm and friendly.

"I talked to Anna and her mother at the hospital last night, and she was definitely in a bad way."

"Aw, honey! I forgot. Your uncle was mixed up in that mess, wasn't he? Is he okay?"

"He was. And that's why I'm here. First and foremost, I'm worried about his safety. Ansel has an officer posted outside his room, but we're worried the person who killed Gable might come after Uncle Monty."

Her brow furrowed. "No. No, no. I can't believe this is happening right in my hometown! First—'scuse my language—that pissant Lance Hilroy ends up dead, and now Gable and your uncle are mixed up in a murder. You just let him come 'round here and I'll show him what's what!" she said fiercely, taking a karate stance. "How's your Uncle Darling? He okay?"

"He's a wreck, and that's why I'm here."

"You want pastries? No, wait! Macarons. Andrew loves pink, strawberry-filled macarons. I'll get you some to bring to him."

I grabbed her arm and smiled. "You're very kind, but like I said, Rhonda, I'm worried about my uncle and the possibility he might know something the killer wants to be sure he doesn't tell anyone…and I can't sit by without at least trying to figure out who did this. So I thought I might ask around about something Anna and her mother told me. It's about Landry Tithers. Does he still work here?"

Immediately, I sensed she became guarded. "He does. He's outside taking a cigarette break right now. Why?"

Instantly, I was on alert. He smoked? Interesting. "Can we speak with him?"

"You don't think…" Rhonda shook her tea towel, her expression one of disgust. "You don't think that boy's mixed up in this mess, do you? He's worked real hard to stay sober, and that's the only reason we hired him. He has to take a drug test every week to stay employed here—no guff allowed about it, neither. I give it to him myself, and he's clean as of last week."

"I'm sure that's true. But I have a couple of questions I'd like to ask anyway. Do you mind?"

"He's right in the back alley. You go on ahead while I fix up a box of those macarons your uncle likes. And if you find something out I oughta know about, you better tell me, Miss Hal. I won't have a druggie workin' here."

"Thanks, Rhonda. I will," I said, giving her arm a squeeze before I headed toward the back exit with Hobbs hot on my heels.

When I pushed open the door, Landry stood by the dumpster, tucked into a dark blue down jacket, his hands and nose beet red. A plume of smoke rose above his head as he stared vacantly at the brick wall in front of him, smoking his cigarette.

"Landry?" I asked, approaching him with tentative steps as Hobbs placed a protective hand on my waist.

He pulled at his knit cap and eyed us with a defensive glare. "Who's askin'?"

I didn't bother to offer my hand, instead I merely responded, "Halliday Valentine, and this is Hobbs Dainty."

He snorted, a puff of condensation shooting from his mouth in a small cloud. "Dainty? Your name is *Dainty*? Like, delicate?"

Hobbs stepped toward Landry, looming over him by at least a foot and a half. "Uh-huh. It rhymes with 'I don't like it when people make fun of my name.' So are you gonna behave like you're still on the playground in fifth grade, or are you gonna use your manners and act like the adult your license says you are?"

I watched Landry's face go even redder before he

straightened up and took a small step backward, but he didn't back down entirely. He made that clear from his defensive tone. "What do you want from me, lady?"

Eyeing him, I jammed my hands in my pockets to keep from putting a hex on his sullen butt. "I want to know what you know about the deaths of Gable Norton and Evan Fowler."

As the snow began to pour out of the sky, he flicked his cigarette to the ground and scrunched up his face. "I don't know anything about either one of them."

"That's not what Patricia Fowler said," Hobbs told him.

"Yeah? Well she's whack, okay?" he spat. "I didn't make Evan take any drugs. I wasn't anywhere around him when he died. They teach you at my substance-abuse program that you're responsible for what you shoot into your veins. Evan shot up a bad batch of somethin'. That's not my fault."

"Did you sell the *bad batch of somethin'* to him, Landry? In fact, while we're talking about selling drugs, did Gable sell drugs for you? Was he still selling them as of last night? Was he only pretending to be clean? Or do you know of someone who might have a drug-related grudge against Gable?" I asked, unconcerned about the accusatory tone to my questions.

Landry's narrowed eyes flashed angry under the bruised purple skies. "What is it with you idiots? It's like you don't want me to get better when every time anything in this Podunk town happens, it's my fault. I'm the first person they come lookin' for. It's crap!"

"Sometimes, your reputation precedes you," Hobbs offered as an explanation.

Landry spat on the ground from a clenched jaw. "Well, I didn't have anything to do with Evan's death. His mother knows that, but she keeps harping about how I'm responsible for getting him into drugs, which is stupid. Evan bought from a lot of people, but I definitely didn't sell him that bad batch of snuff! Evan was a weak little follower who would have taken drugs from the devil himself if he would have invited him to his kegger. It was a long time ago, for crap's sake. Why won't she let it go?"

I fought a cringe at his cavalier attitude about Evan, but I stuck to asking him questions rather than grabbing hold of his ear and dragging him off to the naughty corner.

"How long ago did Evan die, Landry?"

He made a face at me, his cold eyes dull with disinterest. "What? You don't know, lady? What kind of snoop are you? He died almost *eight* years ago—when we were still mostly kids. And before you ask, I don't know if Gable was using drugs again or if anyone from his drug using days was bent enough to want to kill him, but *I* was nowhere near him last night. You can ask Miss Rhonda. I was here working. Now get off my back and leave me alone!" he bellowed.

He made a crude gesture with his finger as he pushed his way past us and stomped back into the bakery.

I looked at Hobbs and made a face as fat flakes of

snow came floating down, hitting my cheeks. "So that was pleasant."

Hobbs clucked his tongue. "He's got a pretty nice-size chip on his shoulder, doesn't he?"

"I want to feel sorry for him because obviously he's the target of a lot of blame, and not without reason, but he was a little bit of a you-know-what. That instantly cancels everything else out."

"Yeah, he was. But he does have an alibi we can check with Rhonda. So let's go check it."

Hobbs held open the door of the bakery for me and motioned to go in ahead of him.

When we entered, I stopped dead in my tracks, my stomach sinking to the floor.

Mothereffer, Hessy Newman—my friendly neighborhood burn-her-at-the-stake fan—was the last person I needed in the mix today. But there was no hiding from her. She saw me the instant we walked out onto the floor of the bakery.

"You!" she yelled, pointing an accusatory finger at me as she backed away, her aging face riddled with lines and creases. "You stay away from me! You're the devil, Halliday Valentine—the devil! Your whole family's wicked!"

Hobbs stared at her for only a moment before he reacted, stepping beside me to put his arm around my waist. "Pardon me, ma'am, is there something we can help you with?"

But I wasn't going to be the shrinking violet here. Plastering a smile on my face, I waved. "Hello, Ms.

Newman. What brings you to Rhonda's today? It's mighty cold out there. Are you grabbing a treat to take home to help you get through the next snowstorm?"

"No, no!" she hissed, backing up farther, her deep-set gray eyes wide. She curled her hands into her pilling red poncho and lifted her chin as though she were facing off with the devil himself. "Don't you come near me with your black magic and your devil's deeds! You stay far away. Far away!"

I take that back. I guess she really did believe I was the devil himself.

What I really wanted to do, as petty as it sounds, was saunter up to her and yell "boo!" in her wrinkly old face, but I knew better. My mother and nana would label that childish. They'd expect me to keep her at arm's length and behave with decorum.

They fear what they don't understand, Hallie-Oop. We have to first try and understand and sympathize with their fear of the unknown before we put up our dukes, I heard my mother's melodic voice say in my head.

But I didn't have to say anything else. Rhonda rushed in and glared at Hessy. "Hessy Newman, you will not treat another customer in my store like that! That's what you're *not* gonna do. No, ma'am. I won't have that nonsense circulating about my friend. Hal's a good person. Now, choose what you'd like and get on out of here!" she hissed with a stern warning.

But I patted her on the arm, turning my back to Hessy, who'd slunk off to the far corner of the bakery, properly chastised. "It's okay, Rhonda, but thank you for being my friend. I appreciate you."

Rhonda gave me a sympathetic look. "She's just old and a little too invested in all that supernatural TV she watches."

I dismissed it with a wave of my hand. "Forget it, Rhonda. She's been saying that all my life. Why I'm here is more important, so can I ask a quick question before I go? Was Landry here last night around five or so?"

"He sure was, honey. He was with me until eight."

Well, there went that suspect. "Thanks, Rhonda. Let's catch up for lunch soon."

And that left us a big fat nowhere.

Landry had all the right attributes, alleged former drug dealer and a smoker who could have possibly held a grudge against Gable. I was sure because the register was untouched and there was no merchandise missing, that Landry had a pretty strong motive to kill Gable if it was about drugs.

Defeated, I dropped a kiss on Rhonda's cheek and began to head toward the door, but she stopped me by holding up her finger. She ran to the far counter and grabbed a couple of rose-gold boxes.

"For your uncle and this handsome Southern boy."

I gave Rhonda a hug and thanked her for the treats before we took our leave and headed back to Hobbs's Jeep.

No sooner were we in the car than he'd set the

boxes on the dashboard and turned to look at me. "Wanna talk about what just happened in there?"

I shook my head. "Nope. It's a long story for another time. Can we unpack it later?"

He stared at me, and if wheels in one's mind existed, his were turning. But he simply smiled and popped open a rose-gold box and sighed with pleasure.

He held up a pink and mint-green confection I didn't know the name of, and smiled. "I like your connections, Lacey. You're kooky cool."

Laughing out loud, I shook my head. "We have to go see Patricia Fowler. I'm not sure what good it will do, or if it'll make any difference, but it's been eight years. That's a long time to keep the flame of anger alive."

"We do have to go see Patricia, and Westcott Morgan" he agreed around a mouthful of cakey goodness as crumbs fell to his jacket and stuck to his closely trimmed beard. "But before we do anything else, you have to try this. It's incredible." He held it up for me to take a bite, but I wrinkled my nose. "Oh, c'mon, just a little taste, Hal. Are you a calorie counter? I mean, it's fine if you are, but you don't need to be. Plus, it's Christmas! What kind of joyless monster says no to treats on Christmas?"

"No. I'm not a calorie counter, I'm—"

He pressed it against my lips and smiled, making me take a bite. My eyes went wide as I cupped my hand under my chin to catch the excess crumbs.

"Wow," I murmured as the vanilla cake with just a hint of orange melted in my mouth.

"See?"

"Fine, fine. You're right. That's incredible. Now, meet up with Westcott then get back to the hospital so we can check on my uncles before we try to find Patricia Fowler, then see who else we can thoroughly offend with our kiddie investigation."

He closed the cardboard box, the treat still in his hand. "Okay, but one more bite, huh?" Hobbs pressed it against my lips again to tempt me with an impish grin. "C'mon. You know you want to."

Laughing, I opened my mouth wide and bit the whole thing, leaving nothing but some frosting dust on his fingertips.

He gasped in mock horror. "Holy tipping cows, young lady. You ate the last bite. No fair!"

I daintily dabbed at the corners of my mouth with my scarf. "All's fair in cake and war."

We both laughed as he pulled out of the parking lot and we headed for our meeting with Westcott Morgan. That felt really good.

Really good.

CHAPTER 10

God Rest Ye Merry Gentlemen
Written by Unknown

*J*ust as we were about to enter the coffee shop, I got a notification on my phone from the local Facebook page, Marshmallow Hollow Chatter.

My heart stopped in my chest as I read a comment from someone about the police finding Kerry Carver's lipstick at Feeney's.

Hobbs looked down at me, his brow furrowed. "Everything okay?"

"Well, all of Marshmallow Hollow knows about Kerry's lipstick the police found at the scene of the crime. They're all talking about it on the page as we speak."

"A leak in the department?" Hobbs wondered out loud, a look of surprise on his face.

"Well, it wasn't me. Was it you?"

He looked me in the eye. "I'd have my skin peeled off at high noon first. So no. Is there an origin to the post? Some proof?"

I didn't believe Hobbs was capable of telling anyone. I mean, who would he tell anyway? He hardly knew anyone. "It says here they heard it on the afternoon news. A leak in the department sounds about right. I sure hope Stiles doesn't think it was us."

"You know what this does, though?"

"What?"

"Gives us a reason to talk to Westcott Morgan."

I leaned back against the coffee shop's brick wall and looked up at his handsome face. "I don't get it."

"What was the reason we were going to give about why we wanted to talk to him about his article? Why would he give two strangers any secret information he might have about the missing girls? But now we can explain we wanted to talk to him about the connection between a missing Kerry, a murdered Gable Norton, and our concerns about the killer coming after Uncle Monty."

That hadn't even occurred to me. That Westcott might want a reason we were so invested in the disappearance of the girls.

I twirled the ends of my hair and batted my eyelashes. "You, Cowboy, have a pretty devious mind. It never occurred to me I'd need a reason to talk to him. I thought he'd just spill all his secrets to me because I'm so cute. What was *your* plan?"

"You are *very* cute, and I was going to wing it. Maybe pretend I was writing a book on serial killers."

I poked him playfully in the chest. "You? Write a book? That's funny, seeing as you've only read one book in your entire life."

"He doesn't know that, silly. And that's not entirely true. I've read other books, but I was forced to read them for school."

Flapping my hands, I rolled my eyes. "I, for one, am glad we don't have to lie. I stink at it," I said before I sneezed.

Hobbs looked at me as though he were affronted at the notion and handed me a tissue. "We weren't going to lie. Only pretend."

"I'm not a very good pretender. Either way, I'm glad we don't have to. Now, are you ready to go find out if Westcott has anything that can help us?"

Hobbs grinned. "Every day, all day." He pulled the door open and motioned for me to go ahead.

I made my way through the rows of tables and booths on either side of the shop, spotting the man who looked like the picture online.

"Westcott Morgan?" I asked of the attractive-looking man, wearing casual jeans and a T-shirt that read, "All Dogs Go to Heaven."

He smiled warm and wide as he rose from the table at Heathrow's Coffee Haus, our local spot for a caffeine fix. "'Tis I," he said with grand flourish. "You're Hal Valentine and Hobbs Dainty?"

"That's us," I said with a return smile as he offered us a seat in the tan vinyl booth with a gesture of his hands.

We slid in, sitting side by side as we looked at this nice-looking guy of about thirty or so with round, black-rimmed glasses, a thatch of curly dark hair, and a bright-white smile.

"Can I get you anything, m'lady? Or you, sir?"

Holding up my hand, I shook my head before pulling a tissue from my pocket to wipe my stuffy nose. I sure hoped I wasn't getting a cold. "I'm fine, thanks."

Hobbs agreed. "Thanks, but I'm good, too."

"So what can I do for you?" he asked before he took a sip of his coffee from a big green mug with snowflakes painted on it.

"We're just curious about the opinion piece you wrote on the missing girls and the connections you made."

He winced. "Yeah, I really stirred up a hornet's nest there, didn't I?"

With a wry smile, I agreed. "Yeah, you really stepped in it. Over fifteen hundred comments and counting."

Westcott gave me a sheepish glance. "Well, what is a journalist without adversary? It's the nature of the beast."

"So what made you choose these cases and question whether the police were picking and choosing importance based on their backgrounds?" Hobbs asked.

"Truthfully? It sort of just fell into my lap, and all I did was spin."

I put my elbow on the table and cupped my chin in my hand. "But tons of people go missing all the time and these girls hardly made a splash, their disappearances didn't even make it to the local news as far as I know. The biggest deal made was on their Facebook pages, and that was from family and friends. What drew your attention to them? How did you find out about them?"

Westcott looked at me thoughtfully for a moment before he answered. "I'm always looking for a scoop. I'm low man on the totem pole at this online only magazine I work for—"

"You work for *The Scene*, right?" I asked.

He smiled and leaned forward, cupping his chin. "Yeah. That's it. And the answer's simple, really. I usually get the fluff pieces. You know, local stuff here and in the surrounding areas like the Christmas tree lighting, the sled races, stuff like that. But I'm always looking to prove myself, move up the ladder, get stories with some meat and potatoes. Call me foolish, but that's how you get ahead in this business. So I do a lot of looking at missing persons cases, murders, you name it, and like I said, this just sort of fell into my lap."

I understood what it was to have to prove your worth. I'd done it when I was an interior designer. I'd scoped out hotels and restaurants, looking for updated décor and presented them to my bosses with my ideas for renovations all the time. It wasn't a bad trait to have, but I got the impression Westcott did it for less altruistic reasons than I had.

Still, I wanted to give him the benefit of the doubt.

Smiling, I nodded, folding my hands in front of me. "I get where you're coming from. I was once young and hungry myself."

He bobbed his head, pushing his glasses up along the bridge of his nose with slender fingers. "Anyway, when I came across the one missing girl, Lisa Simons, the one who's been missing the longest, I didn't think a lot about it other than she was a pretty girl with no leads on her disappearance...but then Jasmine Franks popped up, and man, did she look like Lisa. It made me start looking for more missing girls with similarities. I do a lot of Facebook searches, Twitter, all forms of social media, and that's how I found Kerry Carver, and it blew me out of the water that no one had bothered to put this together. I tried talking to Lisa Simons family, but they wanted no part of me or the article."

"So next you went to Jasmine Franks's mother to see why a bigger deal hadn't been made of her disappearance and why the police weren't doing more?"

He looked at Hobbs, his eyes intense. "Yep, and you know the rest. The police said she'd probably run off with a boyfriend somewhere."

"But you don't think she did?" I asked.

"Oh, I don't know," he said so cavalierly, it was like a kidney punch. "My gut says probably not, but my job isn't to know or not to know. I'm just a lowly investigative journalist trying to get a leg up to bigger things."

So he wasn't invested in their stories—not truly invested—he was only interested in stirring people up.

"So you brought the story to your editor?" Hobbs asked as he unzipped his jacket.

"Yep, and they finally gave me a shot, so I did an opinion piece because the cops didn't seem to be taking their disappearances very seriously. As in, no one had even mentioned the fact that they all disappeared within a thirty- or forty-mile radius of each other, and of course they look a lot alike. I wondered why the police hadn't put it together the way I had. I wondered why it wasn't getting any attention. The economic-class supposition thing just emerged as I wrote it. I mean, were the police deciding one person's life was less important than another's?"

My inner suspicion was this guy wanted to be noticed, and he didn't care how he did it, and even though his questions were valid enough, I didn't feel like he was fighting for truth, justice and the American way.

He didn't come off as totally sleazy, but he didn't exactly come off as a guy who wanted these women found because he gave two hoots. It was just a story to suit his climb up the journalistic ladder and that wasn't sitting well with me.

After that revelation, I just wanted to be done with him. "A fair question indeed. But that's not why we asked you to meet us, Westcott."

He hooked his finger in the handle of the mug, preparing to take another sip. "Why did you?"

"My Uncle Monty," I said, almost perversely enjoying the momentary confused look on his face.

"I don't understand," he said.

"Being the *journalist* you are, I'm sure you heard about the murder at the convenience store out on Snowy Road? Feeney's Fuel and Gruel?"

Then he nodded, pretending he had any sympathy. "I did. Shame. The kid was around my age. Left behind a wife and a baby. What about it?"

"There was someone else involved in the shooting last night. It was my uncle. He had to have major surgery as a result of his involvement."

Now I had his attention. He leaned forward with obvious interest. "I'm sorry, but I still don't know how I can help."

"Have you heard about the police finding Kerry Carver's lipstick at the scene of the crime?"

He blinked and then he swallowed, his throat working. "Holy Cow! I had no idea. How did you find that out?"

"It was all over Facebook, and apparently on this afternoon's news," Hobbs explained.

What kind of investigative journalist didn't keep alerts on Google about the subjects of their stories?

Drumming his long fingers on the table, he asked, "I still don't know how you think I can help?"

I'm not sure what it was about Westcott, but the longer I talked to him, the more I felt like he was no better than Abraham Weller—he just didn't have a law degree. He was an ambulance chaser just like Weller.

Hobbs spoke then, I think sensing my discomfort. "We were hoping you knew something about Kerry Carver's disappearance that you didn't disclose to the public. We realize we're asking you to reveal something you might not yet be ready to reveal, but there's a killer on the loose who needs to be identified. If you have any information that can help us, we'd appreciate it. You never know what might trigger something the police can look into."

"Doesn't your uncle have the answer to that?" he asked, his eyes intense.

He was looking for another story. I felt it. So I clammed up. "I'm not at liberty to discuss my uncle's condition."

Westcott looked at Hobbs for a long moment before he shrugged and said, "Well, everything I put in the article is all I have. I have no idea how Kerry Carver's lipstick is connected to the murder last night, or your uncle's injury. I wish I could help you."

I can't say exactly what it was about him that made my skin itch, but I felt as though someone had unleashed a thousand ants in my pants and I was ready to go.

Westcott Morgan had been a complete waste of time.

Putting my gloves on, I briefly smiled at him as I rose. "Well, thanks for your help. I hope your ploy to climb the ladder of journalistic success doesn't backfire. Take care."

And with that, I didn't even wait for Hobbs. I sauntered through the coffeehouse, the tinkle of Christmas music in my ears as I headed for the door to keep from turning Westcott into a cockroach.

Hobbs caught up with me outside the door, latching onto my arm with a light grip. "Hey, you okay?"

I'm sure my face was red with anger, but I didn't care. "He's no different than that jerk Abraham Weller. He's not interested in the safety of these girls, he's as much an ambulance chaser as Weller is or he would have known about the lipstick leak on the news. He enjoyed the trouble he stirred up. He didn't do it because it was the right thing to do. Whatever happened to journalistic integrity, anyway?"

"I'll give you, he's definitely in it for the salacious side of things."

"Well, it made me want to punch him. I figured I'd better leave before I did and you got the wrong impression about me."

"The impression you're a feisty woman with a big heart?"

I rolled my eyes at him. "No. That mentally I'm a fifth grader with a grudge."

Hobbs tipped his head back and laughed. "How about we go see how Uncle Darling is doing? You know, so we can keep your hands busy?"

I laughed. "You know what they say about idle hands and the devil."

"Then we'd better get your hands elsewhere. STAT," he teased.

As we were turning to leave, I saw Westcott Morgan leave the coffee shop, swallowed up by the crowds of people wandering the sidewalk, looking at the beauty of the decorations, and I had to remind myself it was Christmas.

And in the spirit of the holiday season, I shouldn't turn him into a cockroach.

CHAPTER 11

Little Saint Nick
Written by, Mike Love and Brian Wilson, 1963

$\mathcal{I}$ gave my Uncle Darling a long hug outside Monty's room. Leaning back in his arms, I cupped his cheek with my palm. "How was Uncle Monty feeling?"

He looked exhausted, even after only spending forty-five minutes with my uncle. "He's better."

With such a short, two-word answer, I was almost afraid to ask. "And?"

Uncle Darling grinned his saucy grin as he leaned back against the wall. "And he remembered me."

The look of relief on his face made me sigh in relief, too.

"Yay!" I whisper-yelled so as not to get into trouble

with the nurses who watched everyone with an eagle eye. "That's so great, Uncle Darling."

"But there's bad news."

"*What?*" I asked, a cold shiver slipping along my spine.

"He doesn't remember what happened. And I do mean *nothing*. Nada, zero, zippo, zilch. Not a single second of it after he walked into that bathroom, Hal. The doctor said it might come back to him, that he's had severe trauma, blah, blah, blah, but he also might never remember."

Wrapping an arm around his plump waist, I hugged him to me. "Well, that sucks."

Although, it might be healthier for Uncle Monty to never remember the horror of how he'd ended up on that floor in the men's bathroom of Feeney's.

I prayed my vision was accurate he didn't actually see Gable Norton murdered before his very eyes.

But I didn't want to let on how that *really* sucked, because it also meant Uncle Monty wouldn't be able to help us with any information on what had happened before the killer took Gable out. I'd been hoping he'd at least have something to help us find who did this to him.

"It sure does. Because the police have been here, Hal. Stiles came with them, and they want to question him. If not for Doctor Jordon, they'd have stormed in there and disturbed his recuperation."

I gave him a sympathetic look, smoothing the wrinkles around his eyes with my thumb. "You do know that's standard stuff, don't you? He was knocked out cold in the middle of a crime—a murder. The police are going to want to ask him questions so they can catch the guy who did this. They're not doing it to be meanies, Uncle Darling."

Sighing, he nodded. "Of course I know that, Lamb. Forgive me if I'm easily vapored. I just want him to rest and get better and not have to worry about killers on the loose and those handsome officers grilling him."

"That's why the officer is here. To protect him from killers on the loose." I pointed in the direction of a nice-looking young man with a cup of coffee and newspaper in his lap.

Uncle Darling patted my arm. "Devon is a nice boy. His mother sent cookies for us. He's been very kind. Will you make sure he has a warm lunch?"

I grinned in Devon's direction. "Of course. I'll make sure he's well taken care of. Now, shall we take you home, or is Doctor Jordon going to let you have more time with Uncle Monty?"

His face fell. "Not until tonight, unfortunately. I'd stay all day if they'd let me, in spite of the smell of sanitizer and death."

Sighing at his unfiltered response, I began to steer him toward the elevators when I heard Uncle Monty cry out.

I ran to the room and pushed open the door without thinking, worrying he was hurt. "Uncle Monty, are you all right?"

He reached out to me from the bed, his pale, slender

hand clasping mine. "Hal, oh, Hal…" he murmured with a raspy whisper, and began to cry, pressing my hand to his cheek. "I'm so glad to see you."

I drew his fingers to my lips and pressed a kiss against them, choking back tears at how fragile he looked in the middle of all the machines and needles poked under his pallid skin.

Brushing his weathering cheek with my knuckles, I whispered, "Me, too, Uncle Monty, but I'm not supposed to be in here, especially because I have a case of the sniffles. So hurry and tell me before the nurse comes and boots my butt to the curb, are you okay? What's wrong?"

He pulled me to him, surprisingly strong for someone who'd had such a major surgery. "I remembered something. I have to tell you before I forget."

Uncle Darling came to the other side of the bed, his face a mask of worry. "What is it, my love? Tell me. Do you remember who killed Gable?"

He wrinkled his nose before he coughed. "No. A smell. I remember a smell…"

I think we both stiffened, or at least I did. "What—" I gulped. "What did you smell, Uncle Monty."

"Cigarette smoke. Whoever did this to us—to me and that boy—they smelled like cigarette smoke!"

One of the nurses had come in and given Uncle Monty a sedative when his blood pressure shot through the roof. His condition was such that he needed to be calm and rest, and as I tucked the blanket under his chin and pressed a kiss to his forehead, his words began to jive with me.

That was three of us who'd smelled cigarette smoke. I hadn't revealed my vision to either Monty or Darling, but I did text Stiles and tell him. Maybe the killer had left behind a cigarette butt with DNA. Yet, that felt too easy.

Though, clearly he was a heavy enough smoker for it to have made a lasting impression on my uncle.

Naturally, the doctor was totally against anyone asking questions of Uncle Monty at this point. Delving into that night was going to have to wait until his health was better, but the cigarette smoke was at least something.

Or was it? How many people in the world smoked, anyway? Too many to question about a crime, I'd suppose. I mean, we could go around and ask all the smokers in Marshmallow Hollow questions about Gable's murder, but we'd be at it for a long time to come.

After Uncle Darling said his goodbyes, and as we stood outside Monty's room, preparing to head down the long hallway with its institutional-green colored walls and the attempts to make it look more Christmassy, a man appeared from around the corner.

I recognized him almost immediately. Dean Maverick, attorney-at-law. I saw his commercials all the time on the nights I couldn't sleep and I stayed up watching mindless TV while I sketched décor I hoped to one day create.

His commercials were colorful and loud as he pointed emphatically at the viewers in his knockoff designer suit and promised them a settlement no matter what.

Immediately, I wanted to know why Mr. I'll Get You the Money You Deserve was here.

He sauntered toward me, too confidant, too cocky with his slicked chestnut-brown hair and his expensive suit bought off the backs of people he'd likely roped into his scam of a law practice.

I had to wonder why he was so far from home, too. I thought he was based in Bangor.

"Are you Halliday Valentine?"

My hackles rose almost immediately. "You go grab the elevator, Uncle Darling. I'll meet you downstairs. Hobbs is waiting for you. Tell him I'll be right there." Then I turned to Dean, pretending I didn't know him. Something I sensed would irk his narcissistic personality. "Who's asking?"

There was a slight glimmer of irritation in his hawk-like blue eyes, but he covered it up quickly by sticking his hand out to me. "Dean Maverick. I'm an attorney."

I stared at him without blinking, but I didn't take the hand he offered. "Bully for you."

"And I'm Anna Norton's attorney," he said smugly.

Why the effity-eff would Anna need an attorney? I continued to stare at him with a blank look. "So?"

But he grinned, a devilish upturn of his lips. "So, I'd like to talk to your uncle Montwell Danvers and ask him some questions about what happened last night."

My lips thinned. "Oh."

I knew I was annoying him, but he didn't reveal it in his eyes or even his expression. It was the pulse of the vein in his forehead that gave him away. "May I see him?"

Crossing my arms over my chest, I shook my head. "No. You may not."

"This is a very serious matter, Miss Valentine."

Man, what was it with the greedy slugs these days? After Abraham Weller and Westcott Morgan, I'd had my fill of a peek at the bottom of the barrel.

The nurses behind me stirred from their seats. "So is a subdural hematoma. Go ambulance chase someone gullible enough to believe your cereal-box-prize law degree and fake charming smile."

Dean Maverick's eyes narrowed for the merest of seconds before he tried appealing to me with a different tactic. "A young man is dead, Miss Valentine. I only want to see him get justice."

"And my uncle just had major surgery. So you'll just have to calm your overactive quest to fill your pockets with—"

"And he's been sedated and under strict doctor's orders to rest—without any kind of stress," the nurse who came to stand behind me said. "You're not supposed to be on this floor, Mr. Maverick, and you know it. If you don't leave immediately, I'll have the officer escort you out. You're not disturbing a patient on my watch."

You'd think Dean Maverick would be angry, but instead, he smiled at the nurse as though they were old friends. "Ah, Effie Calloway. Ever the pit bull. That's fine, but I'll be back. Count on it."

He took his time strolling down the hallway, pulling out his phone and stopping by the elevator to scroll through it as if he hadn't just been kicked off the floor.

I turned to Effie Calloway, a tiny redhead with the personality to match her fiery hair, with a smile of relief. "Thank you for that. Are you familiar with him?"

She lifted her chin. "That man is a vulture—the first-scent-of-chum-in-the-water kind of shark lawyer. He gets even a little whiff and he's here, trying to drum up business for that one-man circus he calls a law firm, and I won't have it. You let me know if he shows up again and bothers you, and I'll make sure someone tosses him out on his ear."

I gave her arm a squeeze. "Thank you," I whispered, hanging back while Dean Maverick waited for the elevator to avoid riding down with him.

And I admit. I did something petty I knew Atticus was going to find out about, but I was so filled with disgust, I decided it would be worth it. What was the worst Atti could do?

Ground me? *Me*—a grown woman?

Hah!

I flexed my fingers, placed them under my chin, and wiggled them with a whisper, "Itchy-twitchy, ants in your pants. Do it now, dance, monkey dance!"

As the words left my lips, I took one last glance at Dean Maverick and smiled when a look of surprise came over his face, rather quickly turning to shock only moments before he began to hop around like a cat on a hot tin roof, scratching his unmentionables.

Smiling to myself, I decided to take the elevator at the other end of the hall.

You know, to give Dean his privacy while he itched his way to his next victim, fresh off the ambulance.

CHAPTER 12

O Christmas Tree (O Tannenbaum)
  Written in 1824 by Ernst Anschutz

"*D*inner was really nice, Hobbs. Thanks for cooking. I had no idea hot dogs could be so…festive and fun," I teased as I hunkered down in my favorite full-length coat the color of deep cranberry.

Hobbs laughed at me. "I'll have you know, smoked sausage is not a hot dog. It's a delicacy where I come from, Miss Foodie."

Chuckling, I smiled at him, feeling a little flirtatious. "I'm just teasing. It was the best hot dog I've ever had."

He sighed and shoved his gloved hands into his jacket pockets. "There's just no learnin' you about Southern cuisine, is there?"

Knowing how tired we were from the day's events, Hobbs offered to make dinner for us before we went to the annual Christmas tree lighting in the town square.

And he'd come through in spades. Apparently, my favorite cowboy likes a smoked piece of meat, and he'd thrown some sausage in his smoker before breakfast. He'd also made macaroni and cheese (Southern style), and potato salad.

All were not only welcome, but delicious, leaving both Uncle Darling and me deeply impressed.

Now, as we stood by an outdoor heater waiting for the mayor to light the Christmas tree, I looked for Patricia Fowler. I wasn't sure what we could learn from her. We sure weren't batting a thousand in the suspect department. Evan's death was a long time ago, and though I'm not a mother, I fully understand how the pain of losing a child never goes away.

She was stuck in the time of her son's death, but I didn't really think she had anything to do with Gable's murder, especially with Kerry Carver's lipstick in the mix.

The dots simply didn't connect, but I wanted to talk to her anyway. Maybe she knew someone else who wanted Gable dead, and they knew Kerry Carver? It was the longest of shots, but it was the only scrap I had.

Her most recent Facebook post said she was excited to be meeting her daughter, Cherry, and her grandchildren for the tree lighting. After discussing it with Hobbs, we decided to try to carefully approach her.

The tree lighting in Marshmallow Hollow Square

was something everyone looked forward to each year, and from the looks of it, the falling snow and the bitter cold weather hadn't deterred the locals.

The town had made sure there were plenty of standing heaters and everyone, including us, had bundled up and gathered around them.

I loved the square at Christmas. From the Edison lights hung from the large gazebo where, in the spring and summer, weddings were held and lobster boils were a bi-monthly event, to the evergreen boughs strung around the octagonal-shaped perimeter, it was gorgeous and joyful.

The mayor, Greta Bader, a stout woman with a happy laugh and smiling eyes, tucked into a long coat with a furry collar, was doing the honors tonight. There was a huge digital display with the time and date on it so the children could see how long until Santa arrived from the moment Mayor Bader lit the tree.

We all had battery-operated candles, creating a sea of light. As we waited for the mayor to start the ceremony, I scanned the crowd, looking for Patricia Fowler and her daughter, but hadn't seen them so far.

"Here Comes Santa Claus" played on the sound system while the kids from the high school bell choir played along to the music. The tree, an enormous Douglas fir of at least fifty feet and decorated by the children from the elementary school, sat dark in the center of the square.

Hobbs tipped his cup of hot chocolate, filled to the brim with marshmallows, toward the crowd. "Man, I love seeing all these people. It reminds me of my little town in Texas where most everybody knew everybody."

"Except I bet you guys didn't have to wear ten layers of clothes to keep from getting hypothermia."

Hobbs chuckled as the snow fell around him in fat white flakes. "True. Hey, where's Uncle Darling? I thought he was going to meet us here?"

"He decided he was going to pop in on Uncle Monty and try to catch the lighting from the window of his hospital room. The glow from the tree, if it's clear enough, can be seen from pretty far away."

Hobbs wrinkled his nose as he looked up at the deep velvet of the starless sky. "I dunno if he's going to see much tonight with the snowfall. How about I videotape it with my phone and we show it to him later, so he doesn't entirely miss out?"

I fought a girlish sigh. Hobbs was the nicest, most thoughtful guy I'd ever met. Really. That was the truth. He had it all. Thoughtful, considerate, a gentleman, loved animals, made a killer smoked sausage and mac and cheese, he listened, he communicated. And more than anything, I wanted to trust him with my secret.

Well, at least part of my secret. But for all the amazing things Hobbs is and does, I wondered if he was amazing enough to believe in my visions. They were a huge part of my life, but I had to feel safe enough to share them.

"Kitten?"

I turned to find Stiles smiling down at me, dressed

in a thick jacket and scarf, with an earmuff cap on his head. "Oh, hey, Fitzi! How goes it?"

He put his arm around my shoulders. "Got a second?"

"Yeah, sure." I held up my finger to Hobbs to indicate I needed a minute before letting Stiles lead me to a corner by the gazebo. "What's up?"

"Any more visions?"

"Nope. Other than the one where I smelled cigarette smoke, nothing. Can you believe I suddenly have smell-o-vision?" Then I laughed because the idea was positively absurd.

But he gave me his "quit fooling around, Hal" look. "I've got some new information."

"Are you afraid to share? Because of the lipstick leak?"

Stiles squeezed my shoulder. "I know that wasn't you, Hal. But somebody has a mole. I don't know if it's in Marshmallow Hollow or one of the other stations, but what I *can* tell you is, it's not a good look no matter who has the leak."

Well, at least my best friend in the whole wide world didn't think I was a traitor. "So what's up? I know this is tricky for you, and we can't ever tell your buddies at the station about my visions, but I think you know they've been helpful and that you can trust me. Always. No matter what."

He chucked me under the chin and grinned. "'Course I know that, Kitten. But I have to be careful, is all. I can't afford to be caught, even if I know, without a shadow of a doubt, your visions are never wrong. Otherwise, they'll be labeling *me* the mole."

Rubbing my mitten-covered hands together, I nodded. "Then if you'd rather not tell me, I get it."

"We found a smashed taillight in the parking lot of Feeney's, buried under the snow."

"How does that relate to the crime? It could be anybody's."

His chiseled features held concern. "It has Kerry Carver's skin on it… I don't know how it managed not to end up damaged in the snowfall, but it's her DNA. No doubt."

My blood ran cold. "Holy coconuts. Does that mean she tried to kick her way out of the trunk? Can we hope maybe she got away?" I prayed that was true. I prayed Kerry had put up a bloody stink of a fight.

"That's one theory. We have someone checking the make and model of the car it came from, but it would be a new-ish car. Older cars weren't designed the way they are nowadays, with abductions in mind."

Abductions…

Another chill attacked my spine and my arms, making me shiver. Those missing girls had taken up a fair amount of space in my head, their faces floating around in my mind's eye.

Which reminded me, I needed to tell Stiles about our meeting with that weasel Westcott. Maybe it could help the police with something we'd missed. He'd constructed a possible pattern that at least made sense.

"So are you thinking what I'm thinking?"

He clucked his tongue as people passed by and the excitement for the tree lighting grew. "How about you tell me *what* you're thinking, and I'll tell you if it's what I'm thinking."

I paused for a moment, hoping to get my thoughts together and convey them in full sentences. "Do you think Kerry's abduction was on that SD card or maybe Gable saw her with the killer? But that makes no sense because nothing was reported. I have to believe if Gable thought something was amiss, he'd have called the police, Stiles. But maybe he was somehow in the way of the killer getting the SD card? Like, wrong time, wrong place? I mean, maybe she was in the trunk of the car and the killer realized he'd be caught on camera so he went back the next day to get it? Mr. Feeney did tell you he only checks the tapes every two or three days, right?"

"There's a reason we're BFFs. That's exactly what I was thinking. What we're all thinking at the station, too. Mr. Feeney said because almost nothing happens around Marshmallow Hollow, he doesn't feel like it's necessary to check the tapes that often."

My stomach twisted into a knot. "Any more information from Kerry's parents?"

He sucked his teeth. "Godfrey went to see them today to question them, but they didn't give us much. As far as they're concerned, she's a good girl who would never worry them like this if she could help it. And if we take into account her work ethic from the people she babysat for, and her school records, they're right."

I told him about our meeting with Westcott Morgan and the article he'd written on the disappearance of two more girls before Kerry, but he appeared to know about the others who were missing...he just wasn't *admitting* he knew.

"So you know about the other girls?"

He kept his answer very vague and PC. "We're definitely aware of them and there's a definite pattern, but it's not like anyone's shown up dead. We have no bodies. No leads, according to the police departments in the towns they live in. It's the same story as Kerry Carver's disappearance."

I didn't want to get into Westcott Morgan's accusation against the police. It still made me angry he'd written the article for controversy rather than finding out who'd taken these young women.

Again, my stomach jumped and churned, reminding me I'd had smoked sausage for dinner. "So, what then? They just fell off the face of the Earth?"

"It feels like that sometimes, doesn't it?" Stiles asked, his face grim under the Christmas lights of the gazebo. "Okay, look, that's all I have for now, and you need to go enjoy the Christmas tree lighting with your new love."

"He's not my new love. We're..."

Stiles smiled at me, tucking my hair back under my hat. "Your heart is open but with heavy caution signs flashing because of that slug, Hugo. I get it. I'm just saying, seeing you guys together this last week or so has been nice. You work. I love that for you."

My cheeks flushed and suddenly, even in the bitter cold of twenty degrees, I was warm. "But I have things I have to confess before I can explore this, Stiles. That takes trust."

"I know, and I understand, especially after that dink Hugo. I've got your back, no matter what, Kitten. If you need me to back up you and your visions, I'm there."

I grabbed his hand and gave it a squeeze. "Same goes for me. Now, are we going to watch a Christmas tree lighting or what?"

He laughed at my enthusiasm, knowing full well I loved this part of the Marshmallow Hollow annual festivities. "Go find Hobbs. You should experience his first time seeing it with him, not your boring best friend."

The mayor had just taken her place on the gazebo by the big switch to light the tree. "Come with me," I encouraged with a smile. "We'll all watch together."

I pulled him along behind me, back to where I'd left Hobbs, who had his phone camera ready to take video of the event for Uncle Monty and Darling.

I scoped out the crowd, looking for familiar faces, and happened to see Westcott Morgan and Abraham Weller. Not together, though those two birds should definitely flock together.

No, they were each in different areas. One forced to write about the mundane local Christmas tree lighting, the other probably praying someone was bonked on the head by one of the Christmas ornaments and got a concussion he could turn into a lawsuit.

Mayor Bader grabbed the mic, a screeching sound emitting from it before she spoke, taking my mind completely off those two slugs. "All right, Marshmallow Hollow, are you ready for the fifty-second annual Christmas tree lighting?" she asked, her voice tight with excitement.

We all cheered and whistled our encouragement as the crowd began the countdown. Happy faces shone under the gazebo lights, children danced in excitement, the air was filled with the scent of the ocean, freshly baked cookies and hot pretzels.

I guess I *hadn't* forgotten how much I'd missed this, so much as I'd set it aside in favor of trying to begin a life in a big city. Maybe I'd only tucked it away when I lived in New York. Seeing my friends and employees so joyful, smiles wreathing their faces, I was glad I'd come back. And I was also glad to be sharing this moment with Hobbs.

"Three, two, one!" everyone yelled.

Mayor Bader flipped the switch, illuminating the tree—and it was glorious. Fifty feet of green fir, covered in lights and ornaments the size of soccer balls.

"Now, that's nothing like back home," Hobbs murmured with vivid wonder in his tone and on his handsome face as he smiled at everyone around him, cheering and laughing. "It's like out of a movie."

"It's really something, isn't it?" I said with a happy

sigh, enjoying a brief moment of relief from everything —my uncle's surgery, the worry he'd be hunted down for what he might know, and the tragic death of Gable Norton.

Hobbs gazed down at me, and while a melancholy "I'll Be Home For Christmas" played, the dulcet tones of Karen Carpenter in my ears and the lights from the tree shone down on us, he cupped my cheek and bent down to kiss me…and I rose up on my tiptoes to meet his lips.

It was the briefest of kisses, certainly appropriate for a PDA, but it did things to my toes and my stomach I can't quite put into words. Things I'd never experienced in this way before.

When he pulled away, he smiled down at me, and I got lost in the moment and the warmth of his eyes.

So lost, I almost didn't hear someone scream. Like, *really* let one rip—loud and long—making us all turn to see what the commotion was about.

Right there, in the middle of the crowd of people at the square, a woman collapsed, half-dressed, her remaining clothing torn.

Just crumpled into a heap of tattered limbs and snow.

Both Hobbs and I went running toward her as the crowd backed away. I was the first to get to her, falling to my knees and pulling off my jacket to cover her half-naked body.

Dear Goddess, she was a mess. Her hair was glued to her face, covering her eyes, her body bruised and battered and so very fragile, it hurt to look at her. And her feet were bare and torn to shreds.

"I'll call nine-one-one!" Hobbs yelled over the shrieks of the crowd.

In mere seconds, my fellow townsfolk were taking their coats off to cover her; one mother offered her baby's blanket.

I hauled her up next to me, shivering from the wind that picked up and the falling snowflakes, until Hobbs pulled off his jacket and threw it around my shoulders.

And as I looked down at this battered, bedraggled young woman who hung lifelessly in my arms, her skin like ice, her clothes ripped, I pushed her dark hair from her scratched-up cheek and gasped.

The girl I held in my arms was none other than Kerry Carver.

CHAPTER 13

O Christmas Tree (O Tannenbaum)
Written in 1824 by Ernst Anschutz

Hobbs handed me some hospital coffee from a dispenser he'd gone and found. It was indeed hot, but it was awful. I fought the taste of the bitter liquid as it slipped down my throat.

We sat in the Marshmallow Hollow emergency room lobby, where yet another attempt at decorating for Christmas fell flat against the pale blue walls and pictures of scenic views in town. But I had to admire their attempt to make this place a little more cheerful.

"Are you warm enough, Hal?" Hobbs asked, sliding into the gray seat next to me.

I tucked the hospital blanket around me and

nodded. "I'm good. Have you seen anyone come out yet? I feel like she's been in there for a hundred years."

"No. But she was still alive, Hal. She was still breathing. You have to hang on to that." He took my icy hand in his and rubbed it with his warmer one.

I thought it ironic Hobbs knew exactly how I was feeling, but I rather liked that he understood me that well, so new into our developing relationship.

"I know she was alive, but just barely. She escaped something evil, Hobbs. I know it. But what and who?"

"Realistically, it's going to be a while before we know. While alive, she was in pretty rough shape, Hal. Who knows when the police will be able to talk to her."

That reminded me about the taillight they'd found at Feeney's. "Stiles told me they found a broken tail-light at Feeney's with her DNA on it, Hobbs." That gave me hope; she was a fighter. "Just like the lipstick. Whoever killed Gable had her." I shivered, and this time I couldn't hide the violent shake of my body.

Hobbs wrapped his arm around my shoulders and rubbed my upper arm. "How about I take you home where you can warm up? Maybe take a hot bath and have some decent coffee?"

"No. I'm waiting here until I know she's okay, Hobbs. I'm fine, just chilled to the bone."

The picture of that poor girl, half-dressed and beaten bloody, made me want to curl up in the corner and sob, but I wasn't budging until I knew someone was here for her, and I also knew she was going to be okay. If no one showed up, I'd find a way to make sure I was the face she saw when she woke.

Please, please, please let her wake up.

Hobbs didn't try to change my mind, but he did encourage me to drink my awful coffee. "Drink up. It'll warm you."

The doors of the ER lobby swished open and a middle-aged woman and a man stumbled in, their faces harried, their steps quick.

When they approached the receptionist's desk, the woman—in a gray tweed, thigh-length coat, her eyes tired and hair mussed—gripped the countertop. "We're here for our daughter, Kerry Carver. Where is she? Can we please see her?"

The receptionist shook her head. "Not just yet, Mrs. Carver. Please have a seat, and I promise I'll let you know the minute I know anything, okay? While you do that, can I get you something?"

Mr. Carver bristled, anxious and clearly scared and worried. "My daughter!"

Hobbs rose instantly and called his name. "Mr. Carver? I'm Hobbs Dainty, and this is Hal Valentine. Hal's the one who helped your daughter and kept her warm until the police arrived. Why don't you come sit with us? I'd be happy to get you both something warm to drink—or cold, if you'd prefer."

Mrs. Carver ran toward me, her eyes tear-filled and thick with sorrow as she knelt in front of me. "How did this happen? Is she okay?"

She grabbed my hands, her pleading words tearing

at my heart. I didn't want to mislead them. Kerry had been in pretty bad shape when I was with her, but she'd had a pulse, and though her breathing was feathery and light, she was still alive.

I squeezed her cold hands and looked her in the eye. "We don't know anything yet. She showed up in the middle of the square, and I won't lie to you, she was in pretty rough shape. But she's in good hands, Mrs. Carver. That much I know."

Tears fell from her eyes, splashing against her cheeks and hitting our entwined hands. "Oh, thank Heaven she's alive! Did she say anything? Anything at all?" she asked, her voice hoarse.

"No. She was…unconscious. Am I correct in saying she's been missing for several days now?"

"Five," Mr. Carver ground out, his face distorting from the pain he'd likely experienced these last few days. "Five long, brutal days of wondering and worrying ourselves sick and pacing the floor hour after hour."

My stomach hurt and my heart shook in my chest. I couldn't imagine their terror. "I'm sorry, Mr. Carver. I'm so sorry. But for the moment, or at least when I was with her last, she was okay."

"She must have been…so alone. I can't bear how alone she must have been!" Mrs. Carver choked out as she gripped my hands tighter.

"If it's any consolation, Mrs. Carver, Hal rode with her in the ambulance and made sure she had someone with her at all times until the doctors took her," Hobbs said.

"Thank you," she whispered, her eyes intense as she brought my hands to her chest. "Thank you for being there for our little girl. I can't ever thank you enough!"

"Do you mind if I stay to see how she's doing? I don't want to encroach on you and your husband if it's too upsetting for you."

"Please, stay," Mr. Carver answered.

"How about I see if I can rustle up some coffee for everyone? Or tea?" Hobbs asked.

But Mr. Carver bristled. "We're fine. I just want to see my daughter. Thank you though...Hobbs, is it?"

"Yes, sir."

I'm not sure what made me do it, but I had so many questions spinning around in my head, I had to ask. "Mrs. Carver, can I ask you a question?"

She turned to me, her expression inquisitive. "Of course. Anything."

"Is there anything, anything at all you can tell me about Kerry's disappearance that was unusual, other than her disappearing, of course. Did she behave strangely beforehand? Did the people she babysat for say she'd behaved strangely?"

Mrs. Carver ran her fingers over her temples and squeezed. "Believe me, I've gone over and over this in my head, and I can't think of a single thing that was out of the ordinary."

Every time, it was like hitting the same stinking

wall. "Did Kerry have a boyfriend? Someone she was seeing?"

Instantly, Mrs. Carver sat up straight. "No," she whispered. And then more strongly, "No. She wasn't seeing anyone. She was a good girl. She babysat and she studied and she made good grades. She was a good girl!"

I wasn't aware dating at her age made her less than a good girl, but I got the impression maybe her parents thought differently.

"So you can't think of anyone who would do this to her? I only ask because of the circumstances I'm involved in. I don't know if you're aware, the lipstick they found with Kerry's fingerprints on it was found at the scene of a murder."

Her sigh was ragged. "The police told us when they questioned us, yes."

"My uncle was injured in that murder, but he can't remember anything about that night or the person responsible for killing Gable Norton. And I'm scared to death the murderer is going to come looking for my uncle, thinking he can identify him. I can't impress upon you enough how fearful that leaves me, and I'm convinced whoever took Kerry is the person who killed Gable Norton."

"Oh, you poor thing," she whispered, her face full of sympathy. "I wish I could help but everything I just told you, I told the police, honey. Believe me, I almost *wish* Kerry had a boyfriend so we could pin this on someone, but as I said. She's a good girl."

Hobbs looked at me, and I think he knew what I was thinking.

Kerry was a very good girl…

From the corner of my eye, I saw the ER room doors swish open, but I wasn't paying a great deal of attention until I heard that TV voice.

"Mr. and Mrs. Carver?"

Dean Maverick.

The tips of my ears burned hot as I hopped up from my chair, letting the blanket fall to the floor. "Oh, no you don't, you sleaze!" I whisper-yelled, trying not to disturb the receptionist. "You leave these people alone. They only just got here and already you're looking to poke and prod the child they haven't even been able to see yet? Well, I'm here to tell you, ambulance chaser, not while I'm breathing! Take yourself and your cheap outlet-mall suit right on out of here!" I pointed to the door, my finger shaking with my rage.

But my outburst didn't even lift a hair on Dean Maverick's perfect head. "I have every right to be here, Miss Valentine."

"Did they teach you that in your online class for lawyering?"

His eyes gleamed, as though sparring with me was something he lived for. Dean smiled lasciviously when he said, "My law degree comes from the University of Virginia, just FYI."

"Huh. I didn't know they had online classes."

Now he full-on grinned. "You are very spicy, Ms. Valentine. I like a girl with gusto."

"Do you like a guy who's bigger than you by at least six inches and fifty pounds escorting you from places you're not wanted?" Hobbs asked, looming over him. "I'm going to make a suggestion for a peaceful end to this by asking you to leave." Hobbs hitched his eyes toward the door.

Dean Maverick sized him up and sucked his teeth as he rocked back on his heels. "Easy, big guy. I'm just trying to help the people out and catch a killer."

I nearly blew my head off from the sky-high shot my blood pressure took. "You're doing no such thing. You're looking to cash in on people's pain and get them to sue for some frivolous cause that won't win in even the most three-ring circus of court rooms, all so you can make a buck and bill for nonexistent hours. Go away, Mr. Maverick, or I'm going to call the police and tell them you're harassing people—and then you'd better hope you took the class in how to post your own bail!"

Dean lifted his chin in arrogant defiance, but his smile remained. Unruffled, he pulled a business card from his pocket and held it out to Mrs. Carver. "If you need anything at all, don't hesitate to call."

Oh, the number of bad words I was fighting to keep on the inside right now was off the charts. But I clenched my fists and fought for all the restraint Atti preached.

Mrs. Carver took the card, but she threw it on the ground and, as she looked directly at Dean Maverick, she ground her foot on it and turned her back.

Still, Dean wasn't at all affected. He took his time, strolling out of the emergency room, his tan trench coat swishing about his knees as he did.

"I'm sorry, Mrs. Carver," I apologized. "He's been hanging around, looking to score clients with this whole mess. I'll try to make sure the hospital knows he's been hassling some of us."

"Some of us?" she asked, a worried frown on her face. "Who else is there?"

I explained her daughter's connection to the reasons why Dean Maverick would come sniffing around, excluding the bit about the taillight Stiles told me they'd found, virtually proving she'd been at least in the vicinity of Feeney's.

"The night my uncle was hurt and the night Gable Norton was killed he was hoping to talk to my Uncle Monty because somehow he's roped Anna Norton into making him her attorney."

"Mr. and Mrs. Carver?" asked a tall man with a white doctor's coat and a stethoscope around his neck.

I held my breath when he approached them, praying as hard as I'd ever prayed that Kerry would at least physically be all right.

I backed away, not wanting to intrude, but Mrs. Carver reached for my hand, pulling me toward her. "This is the woman who stayed with my girl in the ambulance. She can hear whatever it is you have to tell us."

Hobbs came to stand by my side, grabbing my other hand and standing close.

"Overall, she's in pretty rough shape. I don't know how long she was out in this weather, but she has some hypothermia that concerns us, aside from her cuts and bruises. She was also dehydrated and exhaustion is certainly a factor. When she came to, we weren't able to calm her down, even after reassuring her she was in the hospital and safe. So we've given her a sedative for the moment, to encourage peaceful rest, and an IV of fluids, and we'll also run some tests. But she's a strong young lady, and physically, her future looks good. You can see her for a bit once she's settled in her room, but I caution you, she's pretty banged up."

I tried to hide the long breath I let out, hissing from my lips like air from a balloon. *Thank you, Goddess.*

I couldn't help it. Tears fell from my eyes as Mr. and Mrs. Carver hugged. And then Mrs. Carver hugged me. "Thank you for taking care of my baby. *Thank you.*"

The Carvers left us to go tend to Kerry—and it was in that moment that everything came crashing down around me. My uncle's surgery, Kerry Carver's condition, looking for a killer in a haystack.

As the quiet settled over me, and the last two days' events seeped in, I dropped my chin to my chest and shuddered an inhale, crying in gratitude and relief.

Hobbs wrapped his arm around me, and I let my head fall to his chest, where I had a good cry.

Today, I'd let all my fear out.

But tomorrow?

Tomorrow I'd take on the day like a fierce warrior

and figure out who did this to my uncle, to Kerry Carver, to Gable Norton.

But that would have to wait until tomorrow.

My phone's loud buzz woke me from a sound sleep. I answered groggily, "Hello?"

"Miss Valentine?"

I sat straight up in bed, my eyes flying open wide. "Yes?"

"This is Belinda Espinoza, from the hospital, do you remember me?"

I scrubbed my eyes with my hand and nodded, then remembered I had to say the word out loud. "Yes, Belinda. I remember. Is everything all right?"

Terror set in, my mouth going dry as I swung my legs over the side of my bed and Atti buzzed to life, flying to my shoulder.

"We need you to come into the hospital, please. We can talk then."

I froze in fear. "Is my uncle…is he all right?"

There was a small hesitation before she said, "Yes. He's all right, but we do need you to come in right away."

"Should I bring his husband with me?" I squeaked, afraid of the answer.

Belinda paused another moment, and then answered, "It might be better if you didn't disturb him."

I looked at the bleached-wood clock above my fireplace and blinked. It was three-thirty in the morning. "Okay, give me ten minutes and I'll be right there."

I jumped off my sleigh bed and went into my bathroom, taking one look at the hair mashed to the side of my face and my puffy eyes, and I didn't care what Atti was going to say about it—I'd frighten the staff of the hospital, looking like this.

Snapping my fingers, I closed my eyes and let my magic do its thing, letting the warmth of it wash over me. My teeth instantly felt clean, my breath was fresh, my hair was brushed and up in a quick topknot, my eyes were no longer puffy and my clothes magically replaced my pajamas.

Atticus instantly buzzed into the bathroom and hovered by my head.

"I'm worried, Atti. The nurse said Uncle Monty was fine, but why would they want me to come in so late at night?"

"I don't know, Poppet. It could be a hundred different things. Don't fret now. Simply stay the course and focus. No panicking until we know there's a reason to do so. Now, shall I come with?"

"No. Stay put in case Uncle Darling wakes up." Snapping my fingers again, I conjured up my favorite boots, looking down to be sure they were tied. "Don't say a word, Atti. Not a word. I'm not going to the hospital looking like I just hopped out of the garbage bin."

"I shan't," he said groggily, his deep voice, so reminiscent of Lou Rawls's, even deeper after slumber. "I'm too tired to fight you, Poppet. In fact, zap yourself over there rather than driving and I shall have your truck waiting for you, toasty and warm in the parking lot when you're finished.

I mock gasped at him in the mirror. "Atti? Are you —are you becoming a softie in your old age?"

"The mere thought gives me the vapors. No, Halliday, I'm becoming exhausted with your constant involvement in the affairs of murder. Now, be on your way, and I shall ensure Andrew stays asleep. I don't imagine you need his brand of dramatics this eve."

I kissed my fingers and smiled at him. "Thanks, Atti. See you in a bit." I gave him a quick stroke on his tiny head and snapped my fingers again—landing squarely on the side of the hospital in the dark parking lot.

I fell out of my transportation spell with a jolt, almost smacking into the brick face of the hospital before I caught myself and faceplanted to the ground.

Squaring my shoulders, I smoothed out my jacket and, as I made my way into the lobby of the hospital, saw that Atti had indeed dropped my truck in the parking lot for me.

With a smile of gratitude, I hit the elevator button for Uncle Monty's floor and stepped inside with a yawn, curious to know what was so urgent.

When I stepped out, I didn't need anyone to tell me what was so urgent. I saw for myself.

The short walk from Uncle Monty's room to the elevator was strewn with all manner of medical debris. A bedpan lie on the floor, along with a toppled cart of medicine, now strewn across the tiles, colorful pills and the tiny plastic cups they divided them into all lining the halls.

I ran to my uncle's room, my feet clapping loudly. Skidding to a halt, I grabbed the doorframe of his room, which was wide open.

His room was also a mess. The chair was toppled over, his TV tray tipped on its side.

And there were drops of blood on the floor.

His bed was surrounded by nurses and a doctor, making my heart crash in hard beats against my ribs.

"What the frack happened?" I had to fight not to scream the words.

"Miss Valentine?" a male voice said from behind.

I whipped around to find a fresh-faced police officer, the one I assumed had been watching my uncle this evening, staring down at me with a serious expression.

"There was an incident."

"An *incident?*"

He nodded curtly. "Someone, dressed as hospital staff, got into your uncle's room and tried to strangle him."

CHAPTER 14

A Holly Jolly Christmas
Written by, Johnny Marks 1965

J sat by my uncle's bed, forcing a smile to my face. His head was still bandaged with more gauze than I thought could possibly exist in all of Marshmallow Hollow, and his arms were bruised from the pokes of the needle for his IV.

"What can I get you, Uncle Monty. Do you need something to drink? More pain meds?"

"I need a fishbowl of tequila and a good Cuban cigar," he groused. If my Uncle Darling was flamboyant and over the top, my Uncle Monty was practical and down-to-earth. He was the calm to Darling's storm.

I ran my hand over the uninjured side of his forehead and giggled. "In light of the fact that Uncle

Darling would probably skin me alive, there'll be no booze for you, buddy, but I promise, if you get better soon, I'll make you a margarita that'll knock your support socks off."

He gurgled a laugh and reached for my hand. "I do love you, kiddo. You know that, right?"

I looked at the angry red marks on his neck and tried to keep my rage in check. "I love you, too, and the next time you want to get me flowers? How about you just ask Uncle Darling to conjure them up?"

He laughed, then put his hand to his head. "Man, that smarts. I don't think the old noggin's ever going to be the same."

"You sacred me to death, Uncle Monty," I whispered with a sniffle.

"I scared me, too. But it's okay, Hal, honey. What would a trip be without a little adventure?"

"I'd prefer your adventures didn't land you in the hospital with major brain surgery."

"I did a million shows on the road with testy drag queens who all have an opinion on their best light. You don't think a little brain surgery's going to get me down, do you?"

I shook my head with a soft laugh. "You need to get some rest, and so do I, because when Uncle Darling finds out someone attacked you, he's going to spit an entire can of glitter hairspray. Now, before I go, can you tell me anything more than you told the police about this attack, or is that all you remember?"

He looked at me with tired eyes. "Just what I told

them, Hal. I didn't see anything until he had his hands around my neck and he was above me. Woke me up from a sound sleep. He wore a mask and one of those surgical caps, too." Uncle Monty shook his head with a wince. "I don't know how I managed to knock that vase of flowers on the nightstand over, but I'm thanking all the forces that be that I did. That nice kid outside came in here like a bat outta Hades. They fought just like you see on those cop shows, but he got away anyhow."

According to the officer in charge of watching after my uncle, the man who'd done this had taken off after a skirmish. The police had searched the perimeter of the hospital and the surrounding areas, but had come up dry.

Of course, there'd be video from the hospital corridors, but how much help could it be if he wore a surgical cap and mask?

But make no mistake. That man wanted to kill my Uncle Monty for what he thought he knew. What he thought Uncle Monty saw. And I wasn't going to let that happen. There had to be some kind of protection spell I could put on him to keep him safe.

Yet, the only one I knew of wouldn't keep him from being strangled, or worse. I was a pretty decent witch given the right circumstances, but I wasn't *that* boss.

"Did he say anything, Uncle Monty? Anything to give us an indication about who he is?"

"Nope, but he smelled like smoke. Just like that night. Remember it clear as day. Has to be the same guy who killed that kid and left me in the shape I'm in."

"And you still can't remember what happened that night…?"

"Not a blankety-blank thing, honey. I'm sorry. I wish I could help," he said groggily. "I heard they brought that girl in here tonight. They're saying she escaped him. Tough little cookie, that one is."

The moment he mentioned Kerry Carver, my heart sped up with worry, even though I knew she was safe because the officer had assured me she and her room were heavily guarded.

Right now, I didn't want to talk about anything other than him getting his rest. "How about you don't worry about anything other than getting better so you can come see all the amazing things I've done at the house."

"Can I go to the bathroom inside now?"

I barked a laugh then covered my mouth. The house had needed some updates, for sure, but not that many.

"You stop, or I'm going to have to accuse you of hanging around Uncle Darling and his flair for thespianism." Leaning in, I gave him a kiss on his cheek. "Now, you sleep, and Darling will be here in the morning. I love you, Uncle Monty."

But his eyes were already closing, his chest rising and falling peacefully.

I tucked the blanket under his chin and tiptoed out to find the officer in charge of looking after my uncle.

He was sitting on the chair again, the hallway no

longer filled with debris, stoically watching his surroundings.

"Hi there. I'm Monty Danvers's niece. Is there anything I can get you? A hot cup of coffee, maybe?"

Blowing out a breath, he shook his head. "No, ma'am. I'm just sitting here feeling really bad that guy got in there in the first place. I'm sure sorry."

But I held up a hand as I read his name tag. "No apology necessary, Officer Little. You can't be expected to know all the staff."

"I wish that made me feel better, but you can bet I'm going to keep an eagle eye on him now. Promise you that."

"I know you will."

"I can't believe they didn't catch him, or maybe I can..." He shook his head in disbelief.

I felt like he needed to vent, so I asked, "What do you mean, maybe you can?"

"He fought like some kind of amped-up ninja—like an expert in something. Never seen anything like it. He was slippery as an eel. Got away from me and never looked back."

"Did you get a good look at him?"

Officer Little gave me a sheepish glance. "I think you know I can't give you that information, Miss Valentine. But I'll be honest when I say I didn't see much. He had on a surgical mask and a cap and he was like some trained attack dog."

I gave him a sympathetic look and shook his hand after thanking him again for looking out for my uncle, realizing there wasn't much he could tell me without creating trouble for himself.

But when I walked down that hall, my stomach was somewhere around my feet. Someone wanted to kill my uncle.

Kill him.

And I had jack squat.

Cigarette smoke, a pink lipstick and an amped-up ninja. What did these three things all have in common?

Nothing.

Absolutely nothing at all.

Covering my mouth as I sneezed, I trudged into the barn where Nana Karen slept peacefully, trying not to wake her. It was still early, but after getting back from the hospital and visiting my Uncle Monty, I figured there was no point in going back to bed.

It was chilly inside, the bales of hay stacked high in the corner, the floor creaking as I looked at the wide-open space with bleary eyes. I'd put a Christmas tree in here for Nana. In fact, we'd decorated it together.

She'd said it was silly, but I reminded her about how it was one of her favorite activities during the holidays, and I missed sharing it with her. She acquiesced, and we'd made a small tree in the corner together one night, while I sipped hot chocolate and let her have one of her beloved candy canes.

It twinkled in the early morning light, soft and white, with some of the decorations I'd made when I was little.

I crept in farther, fighting a sniffle just as the sun was beginning to rise, hoping to get in and out without waking her.

But that wasn't to be. "Mornin', honey," she said groggily, rising to her full height on sleepy legs. "Why you up so early?"

Plopping down on a bale of hay, I rasped a sigh, exhaustion setting in. "It's just been a long night. But I promise to come back later and get you out for some sunshine while it lasts, okay?"

She sniffed the air and honked. "Won't last long, that's for sure. I can smell more snow. How's Monty feeling?"

"Well, he was doing better until this morning, when someone tried to kill him."

Nana gasped and stomped her hooves. "What? Explain yourself, young lady!"

I told her about the prior evening's events with Kerry Carver and Uncle Monty as I turned on the heater and warmed my hands by it while the rising sun slowly crept into the windows of the loft.

"Holy hassenpfeffer," she murmured. "Jiminy, kiddo. I'm sorry you're going through this alone. I wish I could help, but the only magic I had died with me, and as much as you know I love my Andy, he's no kinda support in a time like this. He's too emotional to carry the weight when the problem's his."

I sneezed again, pulling a fresh tissue from my jacket pocket. "But I think you know he's always been there for me. Especially since Mom died. I know he's dramatic and flamboyant and downright over the top, but if the roles were reversed..."

"He'd turn whomever did this into a gooey blob-fish," I heard Atticus say as he buzzed into the barn and landed on the railing of Nana's stall. "And she's not at all alone, Karen. She has me. She will always have me. Speaking of having me, I hear a cold coming on. You should be inside, in a warm bed, with tea and honey, Poppet."

I chuckled and rose to give my familiar a kiss on top of his head. "I'm fine. Just the sniffles. Now, morning, Atticus. How did you sleep?"

"I didn't, Poppet. Once you left, I paced the floors a new hole you'll have to replace. How did the rest of *your* evening fare?"

I winced. "Not great."

"Not great is right. Somebody tried to kill Monty, Atti. What's Marshmallow Hollow coming to?"

Atti didn't even gasp at Nana's words. Instead, he flew to my shoulder and rested his head on my cheek. "Oh, my beautiful girl. Had I known it was so bad, I would have gone with you, mortals be hanged."

Rubbing Nana's soft head, I clucked my tongue. "A bad apple in Marshmallow Hollow doesn't make the entire town bad, Nana. Stop with the doom and gloom. It's just a rough patch."

Now Atti twittered his agreement. "Indeed, Karen. Must you be so gloomy?"

Nana snorted. "This from the gloomiest of 'em all? Hah!" Nuzzling my hand, she asked, "You wanna talk about it, or do you want to just enjoy the peace of this morning before you have to tell Andy what's happened?"

"I wish there were more to tell, Nana. I mean, I have diddly squat in the way of suspects or even evidence, and same for the police. We have a pink lipstick with Kerry Carver's fingerprints on it. A busted taillight from a newer-model car with her DNA, and Uncle Darling's memory that the killer had a nice crease in his pants."

That information made my nana chuckle. "Only my nutty Andy, honey. Only he would remember something so blippin' frivolous."

I rolled my eyes in agreement. "Tell me about it. He also remembers smelling cigarette smoke, and so does Uncle Monty, and so do I because of my vision. Other than that, I've searched Facebook pages and the Twitter accounts of the girls and come up with nothing that would lead me to anyone suspicious, let alone a killer. Yet, I'm sure the person who abducted those girls is the same one who killed Gable Norton. There's no other answer. And it doesn't help that Uncle Monty can't remember a blessed thing. I'm at my wits end, knowing this killer thinks Monty knows something, and I'm worried he'll end up dead like Gable because of it."

That terrified me. I almost couldn't allow myself to think the words.

"And have you tried speaking with the other two girls' families? Friends?" Atti asked.

"That's on my agenda today. Though, I did talk to Kerry Carver's parents, and I get the impression they've kept her pretty sheltered because the most I got out of the conversation was Kerry's a 'very good girl.' As to the other two girls? None of their families have gotten back to me, and I get their reluctance after the police all but throwing their hands in the air, but I'm not going to wait around. I'm going to look them up and go see them."

"What does Hobbs have to say?" Nana asked.

Dabbing at my drippy eyes, I had to give credit where credit was due. "You know, Nana, he's been with me through this whole thing, and I feel like I'm playing dirty pool because I have these visions that can account for a lot of stuff that I can't explain to him. For instance, the cigarette smoke. I can't tell him I smelled the same thing Darling and Monty did, because it happened in my vision, which to a layman sounds positively psychotic and—"

Like a bolt of lightning, in the middle of speaking, the vision hit me, rushing at me in waves of color and sound. My heart slowed its beating, my legs went stiff...and then I saw a man in a dark hoodie with an emblem on the back.

The muffled sound of laughter—no, giggling; a flirty sort of giggle—tinkled in my ears. Then I saw her.

Kerry Carver. She was sitting with the man in the dark hoodie…somewhere… A bookstore? A library? Yes, a library! It was definitely a library. There was a discarded book with a checkout card poking out.

I tried to focus on the emblem on the back of his sweatshirt. Two swords crossed and a letter? Or was that a shape above the swords?

Suddenly, Kerry was in a car and I was in the backseat. She was smiling, laughing, singing to the song on the radio—a Christmas song, "Do You Hear What I Hear?"

And the man reached for her hand, placing it on his lap, bringing it to his lips, kissing her fingertips. If he would only turn around!

Turn around! I tried to yell, knowing it was fruitless.

And then there were screams—raw, afraid. It was dark. We were in the woods, and we were running, and the branches of trees were tearing at my face, slicing my skin. I was cold. So cold, and the harder I ran, the faster the footsteps behind me became.

And all at once, as though someone had sucked all the air out of the room, I was back in the barn, only this time I'd fallen on the floor to my knees and I was gasping for breath.

"Hal!" a male voice called out.

My head spun and my heart raced until I felt Hobbs's hands on my arms, pulling me up and holding me close.

He rested his chin on the top of my head, but his tone held a panicked plea. "Okay, Hal. I'm not falling for the migraine story anymore. Can you please be honest with me about what's goin' on with you when this happens? Are you sick? Is it cancer? A tumor? Somethin' neurological? Don't insult me by pretending it's nothing more than a migraine, because I've looked 'em up, and *nobody* has migraines like this. What's happening?"

It was ridiculous to think I could continue to hide my visions from Hobbs. He was an intelligent man, and the tone in his voice said he was worried. I didn't want him to fret over some medical condition that didn't exist.

I also didn't want him to fret over my being a witch. I wasn't ready to reveal my talking familiar and my reincarnated grandmother.

In that moment, I decided to tell him at least part of the truth.

Patting him on his broad chest, I let loose a long sigh. "I have something to tell you. Let's go inside and talk. You'll want to sit down for this."

CHAPTER 15

Blue Christmas
    Written by Jay W. Johnson and Billy Hayes 1948

---

obbs blinked at me, but not in that you're-completely-out-of-your-gourd way. It was rather like, "I always wondered if psychics were real and here I am, presented with the idea they're real, but it's still a lot to process."

"So no," I finished. "They're not migraines. And if you'd like, I'll prove it to you. Stiles has always known about them, and so does my Uncle Darling. Stiles can tell you that I knew about the pink lipstick without ever going into the bathroom at Feeney's…because I saw it in my vision."

"So the 'migraine' you had at the store that night?

That was a vision of the crime scene with the pink lipstick in it?"

"Yep," I acknowledged. "Also, the smell of cigarette smoke. My uncle can confirm I'd told him about what I'd smelled just before he told me he'd smelled it, too."

He'd sat mostly silent the entire time I told him my story, with the exception of one or two questions, but now he held up a hand. "You don't have to prove anything to me, Hal. I believe you. *Totally.*"

"*Really?*" I cocked my head just before another sneeze came on. "You believe me?" I asked, wiping my watery eyes.

He shrugged, then he smiled. "Why wouldn't I? I mean, you knew things no one could possibly know about the crime scenes. But that does bring up a question. Did you see stuff the last time we fished around a murder—when Lance Hilroy was murdered?"

I gave him a guilty look and sighed. "Yes. I did. I'm sorry I didn't tell you. I wanted to, but it takes a lot of trust… It's why I've never told anyone here in Marshmallow Hollow—because my mother and my grandmother were sure I'd be branded a nut, and they were afraid I'd become an outcast."

His eyes held realization. "Is that what that Hessy Newman was screeching about at the bakery?"

That was a whole other ball of wax. I shrugged. "Sort of. She's definitely put me in the nut category a time or two."

"Then complete honesty, I think your mother and grandmother were right, even though I *still* think you're a little nutty. It's not because you have visions," he teased, reaching across the dining room table for my hand and giving it a squeeze. "I don't care, Hal. It's what makes you Halliday Valentine. That's all I need to know."

My stomach did a little hop, skip and a jump. I didn't know whether to laugh or cry, but I didn't want to dwell. I am who I am, and who I am has visions— among other things.

I braced my hand on my chin. "So I guess you want to know what happened in the barn?"

Hobbs grinned and nodded. "Does the pope wear a funny hat? Does it rain in the rain forest? Do birds fly? Do they poop on your car—"

"Okay, okay," I said with a laugh.

But he held up his hand again. "Only if you want to tell me, Hal. I don't want to pressure you. I was more concerned for your health than anything else."

I snickered. "Not telling you might give me an advantage and leave you firing on one cylinder, Cagney. We can't have that if we're partners, can we? I'll tell you all about it, but first, let me get some coffee. You want some?"

"I reiterate, does the pope wear a funny hat?"

I pushed off from the table. "Coffee it is. Would you check the fire in the fireplace?"

As Hobbs stoked the fire and I grabbed us some coffee from the coffee bar and fed Phil—who was as grouchy as ever when I plopped an unwanted kiss on his head, where he slept atop his cat tree—I told him about what happened with Uncle Monty and my latest vision and that I'd been up since long before dawn.

He sat silent for a moment before he said, "So, the guy had a dark hoodie on and he was in the car with her? What kind of car? Do you know?"

"I have no idea. Maybe it wasn't so much a car as it was the *idea* of a car? In a vision, I see things pretty clearly, but everything was rushing past me fast. That's what made me think car. Plus, there was music. 'Do You Hear What I Hear' was playing, so I assumed it was on a radio. But maybe they were on a train?"

Hobbs took a sip of the coffee I set before him. "You said he was kissing her fingers, right? I thought Kerry's parents claimed she didn't have a boyfriend? Why would he be kissing her fingertips unless they were involved? That seems rather intimate, don't you think?"

"I do think. I think she had a *secret* boyfriend. That's what I think. Did you notice how often her mother said she was such a good girl?"

Hobbs clucked his tongue. "Yeah. I did notice that."

"I think Kerry probably *is* a good girl, but I also think she's the kind of girl who would keep a boyfriend like that a secret *because* she's a good girl, and she doesn't want to disappoint her parents and their expectations. It felt to me like her parents put a certain level of stress on her, maybe about dating and such, that she took very seriously."

"So you think maybe the boyfriend was a bad boy she knew they wouldn't approve of?"

I bit the end of my fingernail. "Maybe."

"I'll tell you what. Let's list what we have and go from there." He fanned out his fingers and began with his index. "We have one pink lipstick that we know is Kerry Carver's because it has her fingerprints on it. We have the smell of cigarette smoke. A crease in his pants, a broken taillight, the sentence 'give me that effin' SD card', three girls missing, a dead guy with an addictive past…"

"And a partridge in a pear tree," I sang. "None of those things add up to much of anything, Hobbs. Like, *nothing*." And the more nothing we had, the more worried I grew.

"Well, let's talk about what you saw in your latest vision. A guy in a hoodie with two swords on the back and a letter or maybe it was an emblem of some kind."

I tried to recall it, but it was all out of whack.

I pulled my laptop toward me and asked Google what sign has two swords, which wasn't much help. "Right, and all Google does is show me stock photos of crossing swords."

"Can you remember the color of the emblem? Or what the letter was?"

I shook my head. "Maybe whatever was above the swords was a shape—some kind of shape." I typed that into Google, but came up dry.

"Maybe it represented a place he'd been or a sports team? But why don't we start acting rather than researching. We can Google stuff like that in the car."

I stared out the window, at the sun gleaming on the snow, and squinted. "So next?"

"How about we talk about the library. How many libraries does Chester Bay have? That feels like a good place to start asking questions, doesn't it?"

I looked up the library and there was only one. "It couldn't hurt to check it out, I guess. I don't know for sure if it was a library in Chester Bay. I only saw an open library book with the checkout index card, but why not? It gives us something to do while we wait to hear from Jasmine Franks's mother and Lisa Simons's parents."

Hobbs stirred in his chair, his anxiousness palpable. "And if they won't come to us, let's go to them. Also, while we're at it, you should tell Stiles about this most recent vision. And something else on the list—seeing Kerry Carver. Do you think we can?"

I shook my head. "She's still unconscious, according to a text from Stiles. The police haven't even been able to talk to her yet."

"Okay. Then it's off to the library and trying to find an address for Jasmine Franks and Lisa Simons," he said with conviction.

Hobbs gave me hope we'd find who wanted to kill my Uncle Monty. He also made me smile. He'd taken my visions as fact, and he had no idea how much that meant.

"You mean, go to the library and show them her picture and see if they can tell us anything?"

"Sure. Why not? There's no law against asking questions." Hobbs was already putting his coat back on.

As I was making sure I turned the coffee pot off and

grabbing my wallet, Uncle Darling woke up and stumbled into the kitchen in his black silk robe and red satin slippers.

"G'morning, Lamb. How are you and your handsome dish today?"

Hobbs chuckled and winked at Uncle Darling. "The dish is good, Uncle Darling. How are *you*?"

He sighed long and dramatically. "Missing my snugglebunny. That's how."

Wincing, I realized I had to tell Uncle Darling about what had happened with Uncle Monty this morning, and that I'd better do it before we headed out to Chester Bay.

Wrapping an arm around his shoulder, I pressed a kiss to his cheek. "Uncle Darling? Let's have a chat before Hobbs and I head out."

"Lamb, are you feeling all right? You sound as stuffy as an old man at an exclusive country club."

Sniffling, I nodded. "I'm fine. But I need to talk to you before we leave. More has happened since last night with Kerry Carver turning up in the square…"

His worried face became *more* worried as I led him to the dining room fireplace and sat him in one of the armchairs while Hobbs fixed him a cup of coffee.

I wasn't looking forward to telling him about the attempt on Uncle Monty's life, and he was likely going to be pretty angry with me that I didn't wake him and bring him with me.

Sucking in a deep breath, I prepared for liftoff.

"He took that like a real champ," Hobbs commented as we sped along the back roads toward Chester Bay library while a light snow pelted the windshield and the torrid blue of the ocean passed us by.

"If you mean he didn't fall dramatically on the floor and clutch his pearls, *that* kind of took it like a champ? Then yes. He took it like a champ, but he was a little peeved with me for not bringing him along. But honestly, I didn't know what was going on until I got to the hospital, and they didn't tell me because they didn't want me driving over in hysterics."

Hobbs gripped the steering wheel. "Why didn't you call me? I would have gone with you, Hal."

"You're very sweet, but it was pretty late. And I know you're a night owl, but are you a three-thirty-in-the-morning kind of night owl?"

He smiled and wiggled his eyebrows. "Sometimes."

Tucking my hands in my lap, I shook my head. "Either way, I didn't want to take a chance on waking you. However, it inspired me to try harder to figure this out. Even if it means being pushy. Whoever did this wants my Uncle Monty dead, because they think he knows something."

As Hobbs drove into the quaint town of Chester Bay, he nodded his agreement. "I'm all for pushy if need be. Now, there's only one library here, you said?"

"Right, and according to GPS, it's three lights into town and a right on Fig Road."

As he looked around, getting his first glimpse of Chester Bay and its cute stores, decorated for Christmas, he said, "It's pretty here, but not as pretty as Marshmallow Hollow."

I looked at the charming stores lining their Main Street and had to agree, it was pretty, with the ocean to the left of us and a lighthouse off in the distance. But they didn't decorate the way we did.

"Really, what *is* as pretty as Marshmallow Hollow at Christmastime—or any time, truthfully?" I asked as he made the right onto Fig Road.

When he turned into the library, a cute little red and white box with ample parking, I sucked in a breath. I found myself a little nervous.

Pulling into a space and putting his Jeep in park, Hobbs reached for my hand. "We're just going to ask some questions."

I took a deep breath and nodded. "You're right. Let's go ask some questions."

Popping open our doors, we hopped out and met at the front of his Jeep, making our way across the snowy parking lot and up the stairs to the heavy wooden double doors boasting a cute Christmas wreath.

It was intensely quiet inside, making me feel guilty for buying most of my reading material online. I remember when visiting the library was a sacred event for me. I adored going to mine in school on my lunch breaks when I was a kid. I loved the scent of old books, the feel of them in my hands, and right then and there, I made a promise to visit Marshmallow Hollow's library more often for my romance novel fixes.

There were a few people scattered amongst the long beige tables and row of computers, with shelf after shelf of books behind them. The carpeting was worn and bland, but the walls held pictures of scenic Chester Bay and some general who'd lived here. Tinsel hung from the front of each aisle of books and there was a display of homemade ornaments, proudly hanging on a tree on the opposite end of the room.

The aisles held only one very serious-looking woman, and another with a pink mohawk and heavy makeup.

As we approached on quiet feet, I smiled at the older woman with a severe gray crewcut, a pencil slim skirt, and prim sweater, and held out my hand. "Hello, I'm Halliday Valentine."

She visibly cringed, backing away. "I don't shake hands. How do I know where your hands have been?"

The girl with the pink mohawk, wearing a T-shirt with the name of a band I didn't recognize on it, rolled her eyes and nudged her. "Jeez, Millie, it's a hand, not a used condom."

I heard Hobbs muffle a snort from behind me and I had to fight a laugh, too, but then I remembered why I was here.

Tucking my hand inside my jacket, I said, "Anyway, I'm Halliday Valentine, and this is Hobbs Dainty. Do you mind if I ask you a question?"

Millie gave me a severe look, her already thin lips thinning further. "What's the question?"

I briefly explained my Uncle Monty's situation and the deal with Kerry Carver, and Millie's overplucked eyebrows rose. "It was all over the news today. How horrible for Kerry and her parents."

"Yeah," the girl with the pink mohawk agreed. "She was always pretty nice. I hope she's gonna be okay. I'm Solange, by the way."

"We do, too," I assured her. "But here's my question. Do you ever remember her coming in here with anyone? Specifically, a man in a hoodie?"

"Kerry Carver with a man?" Millie asked, as if it were a surprise she'd even consider men. "No, never. Why would you ask such a thing? She came in to study —strictly. She was destined for an Ivy League school, not a man."

You'd think I'd asked if she'd come in with a three-eyed monster by the way Millie choked in distaste on the word *man*. I didn't bother to explain to Millie why even someone with a little sense would guess a *man* had beaten Kerry half to death, and that was why I'd asked.

"Then how about this—did you ever see her with anyone at all? Did she ever seem upset?"

The girl with the pink mohawk and bright eyes said, "I did. I saw her with someone. Just once."

Aha.

Now we were getting somewhere.

CHAPTER 16

Hard Candy Christmas
Written by, Carol Hall 1982

"Can you tell us what he looked like?" Hobbs asked, leaning against the shelf of modern history books.

"I didn't see what he looked like," she hastened to add. "I was putting books back and I happened to see her sitting at one of the tables with a guy with a hoodie on, but his back was to me. Their heads were pressed together like they had some big secret, but I didn't see his face. When you said hoodie, it sorta clicked."

My palms grew damp and sweaty. "Here's a crazy question, but it's pertinent, so bear with me. Did you smell smoke? Like, cigarette smoke?"

"There's no smoking in the library," Millie said crossly.

I wrestled with my patience. "I realize that, Millie. But that doesn't mean you can't smell a smoker. Some people are quite sensitive to it. As an example, my uncle is very sensitive to the smell with even just a hint of it."

But Solange shook her head. "He was sort of far away, so I didn't smell anything."

"And how do you know it was Kerry with this man?" Hobbs asked.

"I'd know her laugh anywhere. It's kind of light and tinkling. Like a fairy, ya know? Plus, she was always in here, like Millie said, studying."

I gulped, my throat tight. "So you didn't see his face, but you did see his hoodie, right?"

"Yep," she said with a cluck of her tongue. "He had on a University of Virginia hoodie. I noticed it because it's my dad's alma mater. He played college ball there."

A fizzle of hope bubbled in my stomach. "Can you remember anything else about him? Anything that might be important?"

She rocked back on her high-top sneakers. "I wish I could help you—for Kerry's sake—but that's all I remember."

"Millie?" Hobbs encouraged.

She pursed her lips. "I don't remember her with a man at all. I've told you everything I know. And now, if you'll excuse me, I have work to do." Without another word, she swept off to do said work.

Solange crossed her arms over her chest. "I'm super sorry she's so rude. She's not so bad once you get to know her, but she can come off as kinda snotty at first."

I smiled. But all I could think was, no kidding. "It's fine, Solange. Listen, if you think of anything else, will you give me a call or a text?" I handed her my phone so she could add her number

She bobbed her head, typing in her number. "You bet I will. And hey, if you see Kerry, tell her I said I hope she's okay. And your uncle, too. I hope he's okay, too."

Hobbs nodded at her, putting his hand at my waist. "Thanks, Solange. We'll pass it on."

We didn't have a lot, but we had more than we came in with. The University of Virginia. That was something. Not a lot of something, but something.

As we headed out the door and down the steps, I turned to Hobbs, who had his face buried in his phone as he walked.

"The University of Virginia." Hobbs held up his phone. "Did his hoodie look like this in your vision?" He showed me the emblem for the University of Virginia and I stopped dead in my tracks.

"That's exactly it!" But my excitement quickly faded. "But now what?"

And so what? Now we'd added to our pile of clues with no connections.

"Miss Valentine? Wait! Miss Valentine!"

I turned to find Solange running after us with no coat, her pink hair tipped with the falling snow. "Yes?"

She shivered as the frosty wind blew. "I thought of something else about that guy."

My ears perked up. "What's that?"

"This is gonna sound stupid, but he talked funny. I can't explain it, but it was like he had an accent or something."

How curious. "An accent? British? French?"

"Southern like mine?" Hobbs asked.

But she shrugged as she rubbed her bare arms, now turning red from the cold. "I don't know. I'm not good with stuff like that. I only volunteer here because my dad says it'll look good on my college resume. I'm not much of a reader or anything, and Millie's awful as you already saw, but I put up with it because of my dad. Anyway, I just know he had a weird way of turning a phrase."

I peered at her through the lightly falling snowflakes, my head starting to throb. "Do you remember what he said?"

She wrinkled her freckled nose. "Shoot. I wish I could, but I just remember thinking it was really strange and a little dorky."

Hobbs ran a hand over his jaw. "Did you ever see him come in with anyone else, or just Kerry?"

"Just Kerry. But if I remember what he said or think of anything else, I'll text you, okay? I'd better get back in there or Millie's head's gonna pop right off."

"Go," I ordered with a grateful smile. "It's freezing out here. And thanks, Solange. You've been a big help."

As she turned and ran back into the library, Hobbs

beeped his Jeep. "Talked funny..." he murmured. "That could mean a lot of things."

I squeezed my throbbing temples before blowing my nose. "Yep. It sure could. I only wish I knew what those things were."

He glanced over at me as he positioned his tall frame in the driver's seat. "You're not feeling well, Hal. Let me take you home."

"Not on your life, Cowboy. How do you feel about driving to Jasmine Franks's house in Chowder River and asking her mother some questions she probably won't want to answer?"

He backed out of the parking space and headed out of the library parking lot. "I feel fine about it. It's *you* who doesn't feel fine. And how'd you find an address on her anyway?"

"I didn't." I held up my phone and showed off her Facebook page. "I found the hair salon where she works. She posted on Facebook today and made the mistake of adding her location. So we'll be busting in on her place of work, but it's worth a shot if she gives us something that can help."

He fluffed his hair in comical fashion and batted his eyelashes. "My ends are pretty split, don't you think? I think my ends are split. I think I should get my hair did."

Laughing out loud made me sneeze and groan. "I'll happily buy if you take the hit."

He held out his fist for me to bump. "I still think you should be at home in bed, but go Team Hah."

My brow furrowed and I tucked my jacket around with the sudden onset of the chills. "Hah? What is that?"

"Our names shipped together, silly filly. Hal and Hobbs equals Hah."

That made me laugh so hard I had a coughing fit.

But when I was with Hobbs, I laughed a lot.

So far, no regrets over telling him about my visions.

None at all.

By the time we entered the tiny beauty salon, You Are Hair, in Chowder River, I was feeling right crummy. My head felt like someone had shoved an entire pillow between my ears and my nose dripped like a faucet.

But I was determined to get Jasmine Franks's mother, Sienna—a single parent living paycheck to paycheck, according to the GoFundMe set up for a search for Jasmine—to talk to me.

The salon was small but adorable, with mirrors lining each wall and posters of the latest hair fashions, the smell penetrating even my stuffy nose.

I saw her immediately. A tall, graceful woman with long limbs and shoulder-length hair so dark and shiny, I'd bet I could see my reflection in it. She looked a great deal like Jasmine, who's picture was proudly displayed at her station. They stood side by side, their cheeks pressed together, smiling at what I guessed was her high school graduation.

She smiled at us and waved us back as she finished up with an older woman who headed toward the small receptionist desk, grabbing a broom to sweep the pile of hair on the floor. "Can I help you two?"

"My name is Halliday Valentine, and this is Hobbs Dainty. Is there somewhere private we can talk?"

Instantly, she stiffened, and I can't say as I blame her. I'd bet plenty of people had approached her since Westcott Morgan's article came out.

"About?" she asked, her tone defensive.

"About your daughter and Kerry Carver," Hobbs said.

She blinked, her beautifully made-up eyes instantly suspicious as she leaned against the broom handle. "Are you reporters? Because if you have anything to do with that article, where that chump all but called me Little Orphan Annie, I have nothing to say to you. Nothing at all. I work hard. I'm proud of what I've accomplished. It might not be much, but I've worked for every cent, and I didn't cotton to being called *economically disadvantaged*. I'm not onboard the pity train."

"No, ma'am," Hobbs said, his accent exceptionally pronounced. "It's nothing like that. *Nothing at all.* I'm sure you've heard about the shooting at Feeney's and about Kerry Carver, who turned up last night in Marshmallow Hollow?"

She stopped moving at all then and looked at Hobbs

with less of a glare. "You mean about how they found her lipstick at the convenience store?"

"Yes, ma'am. Hal's uncle was involved in that shooting, which is why we're here."

Thankfully, Hobbs took the reins on this one and explained why we were interrupting her day. When he was done, her entire attitude changed. "I'm so sorry, Miss Valentine. And believe me, I wish I could help, but I don't have much more than I told the police, who, as you know, were about as much help as a poke in the eye."

My heart hurt for her. "And I'm sick to death over that, Miss Franks. I'm sorry you were treated so horribly. I'd like to try and find out as much as I can to help find your daughter and Lisa Simons."

She clucked her tongue at me, jamming her hands in the pockets of her hairdresser's jacket. "To think because she's an adult, she's not worthy of a search party? I couldn't believe my ears, and everything we've done since they basically told me my girl wasn't worth their time has been done by me…by her friends."

"I agree a hundred percent with you," I assured her. "Some of the rules for a missing person are ridiculous, but with Kerry Carver found, maybe she can help."

Her posture relaxed, and her next question told me that she wasn't holding grudges about how the police had handled her daughter's disappearance. "How is she, the poor thing? They said she was pretty beat up."

Hobbs drove his hands into his jacket and shook his

head. "We don't know much yet, Miss Franks. She's still unconscious. But we did learn a thing or two at a library Kerry went to, and we thought maybe if we told you what we learned, it might trigger a memory—something—anything that can help?"

"C'mon to the back where we can sit. You, young lady, look positively green. I've got a cup of hot tea with your name on it."

I *felt* positively green, but I followed her to the back where there was a small table, a refrigerator, and shelves of hair dye and shampoo.

We each took a seat as Hobbs told her about our conversation with Solange while she made me some tea, but Sienna shook her head. "I don't know anything about a boyfriend, or anything like that at all. The police kept making it sound like Jasmine ran off with some boy, but she's a hard worker, her head always in a book. I didn't know about any boys or any men at all. She wants to be a veterinarian, you know. Gracious, that child loved...*loves* animals."

When her voice hitched, I reached for her well-manicured hand, giving it a light squeeze. "I'm sorry to upset you. That's not our intention at all."

She set my tea down and slapped the table with her free hand. "I will not talk about my girl in the past tense. Period."

"And you shouldn't. If Kerry's case is connected to Jasmine and Lisa's, and Kerry got away, Jasmine can, too," I insisted, inhaling the steam of the tea.

Sienna brushed a tear from her eyes. "Darn right,

she can. And my Jasmine's a tough cookie. I promise you that. But I don't have anything more than anyone else does as far as leads go. I've talked to everyone. Her friends at college, her teachers, *everyone*, and they all say the same thing. She wasn't seeing anyone and they never saw her with anyone suspicious."

I wanted to bang my head against the table, but I figured that might be a bit overboard. Yet, these constant roadblocks were infuriating.

"So she never mentioned anyone, never mentioned having any trouble with anyone? Nothing?" I asked.

"Nope," Sienna said, fiddling with the edge of her winter-white turtleneck as though she were thinking about something. And then she sat up ramrod straight. "Wait—did you say the girl at the library said the guy Kerry was with talked *funny*? Was that the word?"

"We did," Hobbs answered.

She put a finger to her chin, and said, "You know, I remember Jazz on the phone with someone. I don't know who it was, but she said they had a way with words that was very *unusual*. Is that the same as funny?"

Both Hobbs and I stopped all motion and looked at each other. Again, it wasn't a lot, but it was something.

"I don't know, Miss Franks," I admitted. "But it's one step closer than we were before. Thank you for talking to us."

And then, in what felt like a desperate, uncharacteristic move, she grabbed my hand again and held firmly.

"Please, please find my little girl! I don't...I don't know if I can go another second without her."

As we rose and said our goodbyes, I gave Sienna a quick hug and promised if we found out anything new, we'd let her know.

While we walked to the car, I had another sneezing fit, making Hobbs give me a concerned look, his eyes filled with worry.

"We're going home, young lady. No more cold and damp snow for you. You need a warm bed, some hot tea, and some chicken soup. Now. And I won't take no for an answer."

I didn't want to agree with him, because I really wanted to talk to Lisa Simons's parents, but with the snow starting to come down as fast as it was, we'd never get to Clemmons City and back home before the roads turned bad anyway.

"Boy, cowboys sure are pushy," I joked as I got in the Jeep.

He smiled at me. "You ain't seen nothin' yet, filly. Just wait until you turn your nose up at my super-duper, fast-acting, cold-curing homemade elixir."

"Huh?"

"You'll see. Tastes like dirt and the sweat of a chimpanzee, but it works, and I'm gonna make you some before I tuck you in, and you're not gonna like it."

Despite how poorly I felt, I laughed. "Dirt and chimpanzee sweat? How do you know what chimpanzee sweat tastes like?"

"You'd be surprised what I know. Now, no more

talk. Dr. Dainty's on duty and he's gonna fix you right up."

That was the last thing I heard before I began to drift off, my last thoughts about the University of Virginia and men who talked funny.

CHAPTER 17

The Christmas Song (Christmas Don't Be Late)
Written by, Ross Bagdasarian 1958

owzers. Hobbs had been right. Whatever he'd put in his super-duper chimpanzee-sweat elixir was heinous, but I did feel a bit better.

He'd brought me inside once we got back and whipped up whatever the stuff that tasted like monkey's butt was, tucked me in, pressed a light kiss to my hot forehead and told me to get some rest, promising to come back and check on me later.

As I glanced at my phone, I saw that it was already almost eight in the evening, I'd slept for four hours, and that meant Nana was going to have my hide if I didn't feed her pronto.

"Halliday, whatever are you doing?" Atti asked, his deep voice warm and soothing.

I slipped off the bed, still a bit lightheaded from Hobbs's elixir. "I'm going to feed Nana Karen, of course. I do it every night, and I'm late. She's going to be very cranky or better known as hangry."

Atti buzzed in front of my face, his long beak, bobbing as he shook his head. "You'll do no such thing. You're quite ill. I'll feed her."

Holding out my finger, I let him land on it and gave him a kiss on his head. "I have some girl talk I need to get off my chest, Atti. No offense to you, but I need a female opinion."

"And must you have that discussion this eve? Can't it wait until you don't sound like a foghorn?"

I wanted to share my elation over Hobbs's acceptance of my visions, and while I was sure Atti would be thrilled for me in his distinctly unaffected, almost bored Atti way, I needed a girl to squeal over it with.

I looked my familiar in the eye. "I'm just a little woozy, but I'm fine. Now, quit haranguing me and let me be a girl for two seconds, huh, grouchy?"

"Ick," he spat. "Far be it from me to keep you from talk of filthy boys. Off with you then. Whilst you're gone, I shall draw a warm bath and stoke the fire."

"Where's Uncle Darling?"

"Visiting Montwell. The doctors allowed them extra time this evening due to how well he's faring. Lovely news, isn't it?"

I grinned and tried to take a sigh of relief, but my tight chest didn't love that. "It sure is."

"Good enough. Now, I'm off to prepare a meal, too. How does chicken and dumplings sound?"

I kissed him on the top of his tiny head again. "Like the best comfort food ever. Thanks, Atti. I love you."

"Ugh, keep your unhealthy slobber to yourself, Miss Witch. Now go, before I change my mind and shackle you to your bed and force you to become well."

Laughing, I headed off to the mudroom to grab my coat and hat and bundle up. I couldn't wait to talk to Nana. I also grabbed my phone and shoved it into the pocket of my jacket.

Pushing the door open, I looked over at Hobbs's cottage and smiled. It was all lit up, courtesy of him. He'd decorated around the rounded door and all across the roofline with red and white Christmas lights. There was a wreath with a big red bow hanging on the door, and he'd even put out a standing wood Santa on the tiny porch, carved and painted by one of our local artisans.

The light was on in his kitchen, which I hoped didn't mean he was cooking up another batch of chimpanzee sweat, but it did make my heart skip a beat that he'd taken such good care of me.

And that reminded me of where we were at this point in the hunt for a killer. Despite the fact that we still had next to nothing, and my uncle was still in danger, I felt as though we'd at least accomplished something.

We had two more clues to this mess. The University of Virginia and a man who talked funny. But was he the same man in both Kerry Carver's case and Jasmine's? Or was that a dumb question? It had to be.

And the U of V was bugging me, but my brain was still fuzzy from whatever Hobbs put in that disgusting drink. *Why* did that sound familiar? Not only because I'd seen the emblem in my vision, but because…

I stopped my short trek to the barn and pulled my phone from my pocket, still on the last Facebook page I'd looked at this afternoon after looking at Jasmine's mother's page.

And several things kept running through my brain, all smushed together and cramming my head at once.

The University of Virginia.

The crease in the killer's pants.

The smell of cigarette smoke.

The description Officer Little had given about the man who'd attacked my uncle.

Solange and Sienna's mention of someone who talked funny…

Holy word so bad, Atti, were I still in grade school, would ground me for a hundred years for saying!

When it all came together, when I pulled up Facebook and double-checked my facts, I instantly texted Stiles to tell him what I thought I knew.

And as luck would have it, that was the instant someone cracked me over the head with something. Something pretty gosh darn hard, thank you very much.

When I opened my eyes, I couldn't focus on where I was because my head hurt so much, it felt like it had been put in a vise grip. I tried to take deep breaths, but my chest, so constricted from congestion, wanted no part of that.

"Hey!" I heard someone whisper and nudge my leg.

Blinking, I tried to see, but it was pitch black and my head was throbbing something fierce.

"Hey! Are you awake?"

A female. It was a female voice. I groaned but managed to say, "Where am I?"

"We don't know," a frightened voice whispered back.

I tried to sit up all the way, but the hard wall to my back scratched at my jacket and kept catching the material. When I attempted to put my hands out in front of me, I found they were chained to something.

My hands were restrained by shackles and icy cold, almost to the point of numb.

Giving a hard tug, I realized I was chained to a wall, which cleared what little fuzziness I had left. Holy schmole.

Stay calm, Halliday. You can get yourself out of any fix if you simply stay calm.

"What's going on?" I asked, even though I was pretty sure I knew what was going on.

"He took you. Just like he took us!"

My heart began to crash against my ribs. "Are you Jasmine and Lisa?"

"Yes!" one girl's voice rang out. "How did you know?"

"Shh, Lisa! Don't be so loud. He'll hear you!" I assumed it was Jasmine giving her the warning.

But I needed to know if I was right. "Who is *he*?"

I figured I already knew, but when you've been bonked on the head and your nose feels like it's going to drip right off your face, and you're chained up somewhere cold and dark, it never hurts to be sure.

"We don't know!" Lisa (I think) cried out, terror in her voice. "He never says anything to us. Not a single word. He always wears that awful Halloween mask every time he comes in here."

"He just throws food at us and a…a bucket for us to…you know," Jasmine said, her husky voice cracking. "And then he leaves again, every single time!"

Then a thought struck sheer terror in me. "He hasn't…"

"No!" they both yelled in unison.

Attempting a sigh of relief, I tried to focus. "Okay, I need you to listen to me. I'm Halliday Valentine—Hal for short. I'm from Marshmallow Hollow, and there are people who've been looking for you. *I've* been looking for you—"

"He killed Kerry!" Lisa squeaked in obvious terror. "I know he did. He dragged her out of here and it feels like weeks since we've seen her! He killed her, and he's going to kill us!"

"It hasn't been weeks since he took her, Lisa," Jasmine reminded her with an edge of irritation to her tone. "Remember? I told you, I've been counting the meals he's been giving us. He feeds us once a day, and it's only been four meals since she left. Only *four*."

The panic in Lisa's voice and the defeat in Jasmine's ripped at my heart. Yet, I sensed Jasmine had been looking out for Lisa, and that gave me a modicum of comfort.

"Lisa! Jasmine! I need you to listen to me. Listen *carefully*. He's not going to kill you, and Kerry's not dead. I promise you, it's all going to be okay. I won't let him hurt you, but you *must* listen."

"Kerry's alive?" Lisa said, her voice watery. "Is that really true?"

"Yes," I whispered. "She's alive. She was pretty beat up, but she's alive. Now listen to me. I'm going to break these chains, and you're going to wonder how, but I can't answer questions now. I need you to promise me you'll let me get you out of here. Promise you'll listen to everything I say. Do it," I ordered.

I could easily break the chains with my magic, but I couldn't afford to waste time while they asked questions I couldn't answer.

An erasure spell was in their near futures, but for now, I needed them to cooperate, and when I got the blankety-blank out of here, I was going to hunt this mothertrucker down and make him rue the day he ever thought up this insane plan.

I desperately wanted to zap us out of here, but I

know my magic only too well. Simple tasks are one thing, zapping all three of us out, when I'm as stressed as I was, could land us somewhere I couldn't keep us safe.

So I'd have to take it one step at a time. *Patience. Patience, Poppet*, I heard Atti say in my head.

Closing my eyes, I said again, "Ladies? Do you hear me? I'm going to get you out of here, but it's crucial you listen to me."

"But how—"

"Lisa!" Jasmine chastised. "She said don't ask questions. Do you want to be in here forever? Or do you want to go home to your cat, Seamus?"

That gave me a talking point, something to distract them. "You have a cat, Lisa? Me too. His name's Phil. Mine's a total jerk. Super aloof, hates any kind of affection unless it's on his terms…and to think, I rescued him. What's yours like?" I asked as I rubbed my fingertips together and twisted my wrists.

As Lisa began describing her cat, I focused on freeing myself. My trusty magic surged through me in a tidal wave of blissful power, popping first one cuff and then the next.

Finally free, but unable to see a bloody thing, I felt around.

The floor was dirt, and cold, but when I reached out, I felt material. A blanket? Then something soft that almost had me recoiling until I realized it was a pillow.

With my pulse racing, I called out, "Jasmine, talk to

me. I can't see a thing. I need to follow the sound of your voice."

"My name is Jasmine Franks, and I want to go home, Hal. I want to go home so bad, I can't even tell you. I…I miss my mother. I miss my dog Juniper. She's a rescue. A French bulldog, and she sleeps with me every night. I…I miss her…" she sobbed softly.

I began crawling, my hands touching every inch of the surface between myself and Jasmine's voice. "I saw your mother today, Jasmine. She misses you so much. She's going to be so happy you're okay."

I heard her gasp softly. "You saw her? Is she okay?"

"She's fine, Jasmine. She just misses you, but not for long," I said as I struggled to bridge the gap between us. When I finally touched flesh, I asked, "Is that your ankle?"

"Yes. Oh, thank God, yes!"

"Hold your hands out to me, Jasmine. Reach for mine." When I felt her fingers touch mine, I worked my way along her hands until I gripped her wrists, and she began to openly weep. "Hush now, Jasmine," I soothed, stroking her arm. "I know you've been locked away here a long time, but I'm begging you, listen to me. I need you to stay calm, and I promise I'll get you out. I swear it. If it's the last thing I do, I'll get you home to your mother and Juniper."

The last thing I needed was for my magic to go kerflooey due to my stress. Rather than succumb to her soft sobs, I focused on the feel of the shackles and

Jasmine's icy fingers—and to my sheer delight, her cuffs fell off and clanked to the ground.

"How did you...?"

Hearing the awe and wonder in her voice, the relief, almost made me tear up. Being here so long must have been a living nightmare, but I couldn't afford to lose my focus.

"No questions!" I all but yelled. "Lisa? Now you, sweetie. Talk to me. Tell me what your favorite subject was in school. It was art, right?"

I think I recalled that detail from her Facebook page.

As Lisa began to talk about her art class, and the teacher she'd so admired, it was easy to find her. The room was quite small, and when I walked my way up her legs, I grabbed onto her wrists, rubbing the smooth metal of the thick cuffs until they fell away like melted butter.

Sitting back on my haunches, I took as deep a breath as my congestion would allow while I thought about how I was going to do this without them losing their minds and becoming what I most feared.

Afraid of me.

I wanted to zap us out of here, but my fear was the same as it's always been. What if I was so stressed, my magic failed and we ended up in the outer regions of Mongolia—or worse, another dimension? I wanted to trust myself, but I'd done worse under far less stressful circumstances.

Or what if they became afraid of me and my powers

and they flipped? I couldn't afford for them to become hysterical.

Licking my dry lips, and flexing my icy-cold fingers, I said, "I need you both to listen to me and I mean truly listen. I'm going to do something that's going to—"

But I didn't have time to finish that sentence before a heavy metal door burst open—and there in the very pale light of a quarter moon stood the repulsive scumbag who'd started this whole thing...all for a leg up.

Westcott Morgan.

CHAPTER 18

Mistletoe
  Written by, Nasri, Justin Bieber, Adam Messinger
2011

$\mathcal{A}$nd Westcott Morgan had a really big gun.

Now, I've said this before, I don't know a whole lot about guns, but I think it was Mr. Feeney's shotgun, and all I can tell you is this: no matter the cost, I wasn't going to let these girls end up with big ugly holes in their chests the way Gable had.

Both of the girls cried out in what sounded like surprise and, of course, terror, but I shoved them behind me as my eyes adjusted to the light and the wind rushed in, blowing snowflakes directly into my face.

"*You!*" he seethed. "Why couldn't you just leave well enough alone? Why couldn't you just go away?!"

From the kneeling position I was in, Jasmine and Lisa clung to me, their bodies trembling so violently, I almost tipped over.

Yet, I countered, my head throbbing, my eyes fixed on the barrel of that gun. "Why did you murder Gable Norton? How did that fit into your sick plan to manufacture a big story?"

Because, BTW, that's what he'd done. He'd manufactured this entire mess from start to finish.

His nostrils flared, his eyes wild and his face distorted as he cried, "I didn't mean to kill him! That was never part of the plan! *Never!* If he'd have just given me the SD card, I would have left and no one would have gotten hurt! I just wanted to prove I could write a story! I swear I was going to bring them all back. No one was supposed to get hurt!"

My seething anger, my disgust, took over as I clenched my fists. "Isn't there something about the best-laid plans, Westcott? You're a writer," I spat. "You know what I mean, don't you, wordsmith? But in your quest for a story, you almost killed my uncle!"

Jasmine and Lisa whimpered behind me, but I held them back.

Westcott Morgan's face crumbled at my words, but he had a firm grip on that gun. "I didn't know he was in the bathroom! I swear, I didn't know, Hal! I was fighting with Gable, and then your uncle was on the floor bleeding and Gable had a hole in his chest the size of a donut! I didn't mean for anyone to get hurt!"

I rose on slow legs, aching and tried from kneeling. "Why did you want the SD card, Westcott? What was on it that you didn't want anyone to see?"

His shoulders slumped as the wind tore at his curly hair and his eyes went dull. "I was going to dump Kerry that night—maybe in the woods. I wasn't going to hurt her. I wasn't going to hurt *any* of them. I swear it! But Kerry got away. She got out of the trunk of my car. I didn't give her enough of the sedative. I knew I should have given her more!"

My pulse raced as I decided I didn't care *where* we were transported to, as long as we got away from this maniac. If only I could remember the words…

"And she got away from you, didn't she, Westcott? She ran away and hid in the woods for two days!"

He nodded a sad bob of his head as he steadied the gun. "She ran off…and it was all going to be on that SD card, Hal. All of it. Every single second of me going into the store to get her food while she broke out of the trunk. I was going in there so I could leave her with food, and she ran away!"

The way he said those words, as though I should pity him because he was going to feed his *hostage*—his *victim*—made my stomach roll. I'm pretty sure some of that upset had to do with the gunk Hobbs had given me, but I felt like I was on a Tilt-A-Whirl.

"And then what, Westcott? What were you going to do then?"

He shook his head, his eyes wild. "I don't know!" he moaned. "They didn't know who I was. The only person who knew was your uncle because when I was fighting with Gable, he pulled up my mask. I was careful, Hal. I was always careful when I brought them food. When I drugged them. I was *so* careful!"

The wind tore at my jacket, slashing at my face, but I wanted blood. I wanted him to suffer the way he'd allowed their parents and my uncle to suffer.

"And you were going to be the hero, weren't you, Westcott Morgan?" I sneered his name. "You were going to dump them somewhere and find them, bring them home, and then you could be the hero of the story *you* created! That's what you were going to do. You're repulsive!"

His breathing shifted to almost a pant. "I just wanted a story. A good story. That's all. I didn't mean for anyone to get hurt!"

"And now what, Westcott? What are you going to do with us now? *Shoot us?*" I asked, baiting him, knowing it would frighten the girls but doing it anyway.

His eyes grew round and wide, filling with the tears of a man in way over his head. "I don't have a choice, Hal. *You've* left me no choice. Don't you see? I can't let you live! You asked too many questions. Too many! You saw Jasmine's mother. You were at the library today... That's where I first got the idea for this crazy plan. While I was sitting there with Kerry, just talking about nothing."

As much as I wanted to stroll down memory lane with him, right now, I only wanted out—and I needed but a moment's peace to get there. I could have the answers to my questions later.

I leered at him, making my eyes go wide and turning my mouth into a grimace of disgust, hoping to incite him. "So do it, Westcott. *Do it, you coward!*" I moved closer as he pointed that gun at me under the light of the moon. "Kill us, you sad sack of horse dung! Kill us all!" I screamed, spit flying from my mouth.

The moment of surprise in his eyes was the moment I needed to bellow, "Strength of ten men, draw me near, save me from the thing I fear!"

With those words, words I prayed were right, I ran at Westcott with everything I had, steamrolling him square in the middle of his stomach with the top of my stuffed-up head.

As he doubled over and fell to the ground as though a wrecking ball had rammed into him, and I fell on top of him, I roared, "Run, girls! Run, and don't stop running until you find help!"

I heard the thunder of feet behind me just as Westcott was recuperating, and I knew, in this vacuum of stress, I had to stop him physically, because a spell was an even riskier proposition than it had been two seconds ago.

He jammed his fingers into my cheekbones, latching onto my face and screaming his rage, throwing me from him. I landed in the snow, hard-packed and like knives in my back.

I had no idea where we were, no earthly idea other than the flash of trees I saw as he tossed me off him.

My head cracked against something hard, leaving me on my side with the wind knocked out of me. Snow pelted my face, the wind ate at my skin, my body ached.

And then I saw Westcott's hands reaching for the gun, his arms stretching, the grunts of his struggle ringing in my ears.

So look, I don't know how else to explain this other than I'd just binge-watched *Game of Thrones* (yes, I know. I was way late to the party. But better late than never), and in my crazy mixed-up panic, I saw Jason Momoa's character, Khal Drogo, in my head.

That was only seconds before I yelped, my ribs burning from the effort, "Westcott, no!"

He looked to me—and what had once been grit and determination in his gaze was now complete terror.

"*How?*" he screeched in abject fear.

Again, I don't know how I did it, but I guess I'd conjured up Khal Drogo's face instead of a transportation spell.

No, cloaking yourself in someone else's countenance isn't even remotely like a transportation spell. I get that. But I worked with what I had and tried not to laugh out loud at the idea of Jason Momoa's head on my short little body.

Westcott's disbelief gave me enough time to scramble to my feet and grab the gun. Huffing and puffing, I clung to it and pointed it at his chest.

Gasping for air, I managed to order, "Don't move, or I swear on Daenerys Targaryen, I'll shoot you!"

"Oh, Kitten. What have you done?" Stiles asked me with a smile.

Sitting on the edge of the ambulance's backend, I pulled the warm blanket around my shoulders and shrugged. "Let's just say, I don't think Westcott's a fan of *Game of Thrones.*"

"And can you fix that?" he asked under his breath. "Because he's carrying on something fierce about, of all things, Jason Momoa."

I looked up at him, my eyes grainy and tired. "I can, but let me enjoy the moment for just a little longer, will you?"

"I can't believe you figured it out."

Shaking my head, I snorted. "And again, I was a day late and a dollar short. I would have preferred to find him, tell you, and avoid being concussed."

Stiles laughed. "You can't blame yourself for the fact that he whacked you over the head before you could tell me."

"You're right. I did figure it out before he whacked me over the head and drugged me, and I was going to text it all to you so you could arrest him, and instead, I ended up in shackles in some weird half-underground shed in the deepest origins of the woods with a likely concussion and the worst stuffy nose ever."

Stiles laughed and pulled me to his chest for a quick hug. "How did you figure it out, anyway?"

I couldn't wait to tell my sister Stevie, a crime-solving expert, that I'd actually figured out a crime. "It was a combo pack of whammies. That University of Virginia thing was sticking to me like glue, but then I remembered that was because Dean Maverick had mentioned it's where he got his law degree. So at first I thought it was him, you know, creating a crime to cash in on some lawsuits."

"But?" Stiles asked, his eyebrows raised as he tightened the blanket around me.

"But while he's a total tool, the talking-funny thing and the smell of cigarette smoke didn't jive with him. Though, the crease in his pants sure fit. He does like a nice cheap suit."

Stiles brow furrowed. "Still don't know where you're going with this, Hal."

"Talking funny was what made me check Westcott Morgan's page on Facebook. He's a writer. They know all sorts of words and phrases unique to other countries, right?"

"Right..."

I shrugged. "He called me m'lady when we first met, and used the words *'tis I* when he introduced himself. That was what made me suspicious, but when I got to his page, there was a picture of him at his friend's wedding the night of Gable's murder—and he had on a suit with creased pants and a cigarette in his hand. Lots of people smoke when they're stressed, right? And I'd suppose he was pretty stressed after kidnapping three women and holding them hostage, but he was probably *especially* stressed when he went to get that SD card, and in the process of moving Kerry so he could dump her and look like a hero, she got away."

Stiles blew out a long breath and rubbed his hands together. "I still don't know how the heck she survived out here in the bitter cold for two days."

I shivered, so grateful she had. "Me neither, but miracles happen all the time, Stiles. All the time."

He gave me a light nudge. "That's fair. Is there more I should know? You know, in case someone asks me how you figured this out?"

"Well, coincidence would have it that Westcott went to the University of Virginia, too, and he's pretty skilled at taekwondo, which explains what Officer Little said about the guy who attacked Uncle Monty."

A look of realization came over Stiles's face. "Ohhh, he said he fought like an amped-up ninja, right? He couldn't stop talking about how the department should pay for us to have classes in martial arts."

"Well," I teased, "he *did* get away…"

Stiles paused for a second and then he pulled his phone from his pocket and said, "So lover boy's blowing up my phone right now, worried sick about you. I say we call it a night, and get you back to him before he blows a gasket next."

My heart smiled at that. Right there in my chest.

Chuckling, I asked, "Do you think the officers need anything else for tonight, because I feel like poop and they look like they have their hands full with Westcott and his carrying on about Jason Momoa."

"Um, yeah, could you fix that so he forgets, because you're my best friend and everyone in the department knows it. They're going to start asking questions. And while you're at it, fix the girls' memories, too."

I snapped my fingers, the warmth of my magic surging through my veins. "There. All done. But I have one last question for you."

"That is?"

"How am I supposed to explain how I got us out of those shackles?"

He grinned. "Bobby pins, Kitten. Lots of bobby pins."

"Oooh, yours is really nice, Hobbs," I complimented. "For a boy from Texas, you're all right."

He grinned his devastatingly handsome grin. "I admit, it's a pretty good one."

We were lying side by side on the ground in the snow, beneath the big oak tree in my backyard, covered in Christmas lights at ten o'clock at night, staring at the stars and making snow angels and laughing like silly teenagers.

I was feeling much better, and the knock to my head from Westcott Morgan didn't hurt so much anymore, though I did still have an ugly knot.

My Uncle Monty was due out of the hospital at the end of the week, and Uncle Darling had decided to extend their stay another couple of days so we could baby Monty and give him all the love he so deserved.

Hobbs stopped moving his arms and looked over at me. "So how was Kerry today?"

I sighed. There was a lot of trauma there. Trauma that would take time to heal, no doubt. "She's better. Still shaky, but better."

Kerry had asked to see me when she found out I was the person who'd stayed with her in the ambulance, and I'd agreed.

When I first saw her, thin and pale but with a semi-smile, I almost burst into tears, I was so glad she was awake. When she told me the chilling story of how she'd met Westcott Morgan, when she'd relayed how he'd lured her in, I could do nothing but be there for her in silent horror.

"Did she tell you how she met Westcott?"

"At a coffee shop in Chester Bay. They'd been dating about a week before he kidnapped her. But she didn't know it was him who'd grabbed her, by the way. He wore a Halloween mask and he injected her with a mild sedative."

Hobbs's lips thinned. "I don't understand what he was going to do with her. Why did he take her from the shed in the first place?"

"Well, from what Stiles said, by the time he took Kerry, he was already feeling the weight of what he'd done. The snowball effect of having to keep these women alive and fed and keep himself out of trouble was getting to be a lot. He was getting scared. Things got really out of hand when my uncle saw him. He still doesn't remember that night, but of course, Westcott didn't know that."

Uncle Monty, when showed Westcott's picture, couldn't remember him at all.

"So he was going to get rid of her. That's why she was in the trunk of the car that night, but they were caught on camera, and that's why he needed the SD card."

I nodded my head. "That was the plan. He didn't want to kill her, according to his statement. He just wanted to get rid of her so he was in the clear. So he roughed her up, drugged her, and threw her in the trunk. He was going to do the same thing with Jasmine and Lisa. Like I said, I think what really happened was, he got in too deep and he couldn't get back out. So his solution was to ditch them and run, but he knew when Kerry escaped, the night he planned to dump her somewhere off the interstate, that his image would be on that SD card."

Hobbs sighed, folding his hands over his flat belly. "So he went back to get it, so there'd be no evidence; got caught up with Gable, who he didn't expect to pull a shotgun on him; got into a fight, managed to get the gun, and shot him?"

I flapped my arms in the cold snow. "And knocked Uncle Monty out cold—but not before Gable managed to pull off his mask. Uh-huh. That's how it went down."

"Remember you mentioned Anna said Gable seemed agitated and she thought he was drinking again, but he didn't smell like alcohol? Do you think he saw something the night Kerry escaped?"

"Actually, Stiles told me they suspect it was probably because Mr. Feeney had offered Gable a partnership in the store and he was nervous and excited and wanted to surprise Anna with the news. Mr. Feeney was looking to retire and Anna found the papers with the offer in Gable's desk when she was going through it for their life insurance policy."

The disgust in Hobbs's voice was evident. "Man, what a shame for Anna and Gable. And Westcott did all that to create a story big enough to get himself noticed?"

"One he hoped would go national and gain him the notoriety he so desperately craved. Sort of like the guy who starts fires and is the first one on the scene to put them out, then comes off looking like a hero."

Hobbs scoffed. "That duplicitous little weasel. When I think about the effort that took. I mean, he chose girls who not only looked similar, but had similar backgrounds, two of whom he basically wooed."

Nodding, I stopped flapping my arms because they still hurt after my struggle with Westcott. "Jasmine claims the reason she gave him her number after she'd first met him was because he was, in her words, chivalrous. That's who she was talking to on the phone when her mother overheard."

"But she didn't go out with him, right? Only Kerry did?"

I stared up at the lights on the icy fingers of the tree. "Right. He asked, but Jasmine declined due to heavy schoolwork. Kerry was besotted with him after a couple of dates, then he kidnapped her."

"Basically, he groomed her." He shivered. "How thoroughly chilling."

"Tell me about it," I muttered. "But the good news is, he didn't hurt the girls…if you know what I mean…"

Hobbs stopped flapping his arms and rolled to his side to look at me. "I do know what you mean, and I'm grateful they won't have that on their plates, too."

"Me too. And what a Christmas gift to have all three girls safe and home. I'm so grateful." *So grateful.*

"So the ladies have reported you were pretty brave, Ms. Hal."

I rolled to my side, as well. "That's ridiculous. I just distracted him long enough for them to get away."

"While you held him at gunpoint and called the police with *his* phone. How did you get the gun away from him?" The pride in his voice made me blush.

That was a story for another day.

Instead, I smiled at him. "Yoga."

"I'd like for you to teach me some of that brand of yoga."

"Do you think you'll be held at gunpoint anytime soon, Cowboy?"

"Well, we *are* two for two."

"Nuh-uh, Cowboy. *I'm* two for two. You're one for two," I teased with a poke to his arm.

He chuckled, deep and resonant. "Hey, know what?"

I knew I wanted to ask him what he thought the typewriter in my visions was all about—something we still hadn't discussed. That's what. But the look in his eyes said it could wait.

"What?"

"I'm really glad you're okay."

"I'm really glad I'm okay, too."

"And *now* you know what?"

"What?"

"I'm going to kiss you. That's what."

And he did.

Phew, did he ever.

THE END

Thank you for joining Hal and her pals for *Have Yourself a Merry Little Witness*, I hope you'll come back for book three titled, *One Corpse Open Slay*!

NOTE FROM DAKOTA CASSIDY

I do hope you enjoyed this book, I'd so appreciate it if you'd help others enjoy it too.

Recommend it. Please help other readers find this book by recommending it.

Review it. Please tell other readers why you liked this book by reviewing it at online retailers or your blog. Reader reviews help my books continue to be valued by distributors/resellers. I adore each and every reader who takes the time to write one!

ABOUT THE AUTHOR

Dakota Cassidy is a USA Today bestselling author with over eighty books. She writes laugh-out-loud cozy mysteries, romantic comedy, grab-some-ice erotic romance, hot and sexy alpha males, paranormal shifters, contemporary kick-butt women, and more.

She received a starred review from Publishers Weekly for Talk Dirty to Me, won a Romantic Times Reviewers' Choice Award for Kiss and Hell, along with many review site recommended reads and reviewer top pick awards.

Dakota lives in the gorgeous state of Oregon with her real-life hero and her dogs, and she loves hearing from readers!

Visit Dakota's website at http://www. dakotacassidy.com for more information.

A Lemon Layne Mystery, a Contemporary Cozy Mystery Series

    1. Prawn of the Dead

    2. Play That Funky Music White Koi

Witchless In Seattle Mysteries, a Paranormal Cozy Mystery series

    1. Witch Slapped

    2. Quit Your Witchin'

    3. Dewitched

    4. The Old Witcheroo

    5. How the Witch Stole Christmas

    6. Ain't Love a Witch

    7. Good Witch Hunting

    8. Witch Way Did He Go?

    9. Witches Get Stitches

10. Witch it Real Good
11. Witch Perfect
12. Gettin' Witched

Marshmallow Hollow Mysteries, a Paranormal Cozy Mystery series

1. Jingle all the Slay
2. Have Yourself a Merry Little Witness

Nun of Your Business Mysteries, a Paranormal Cozy Mystery series

1. Then There Were Nun
2. Hit and Nun
3. House of the Rising Nun
4. The Smoking Nun
5. What a Nunderful World

Wolf Mates, a Paranormal Romantic Comedy series

1. An American Werewolf In Hoboken
2. What's New, Pussycat?
3. Gotta Have Faith
4. Moves Like Jagger
5. Bad Case of Loving You

A Paris, Texas Romance, a Paranormal Romantic Comedy series

1. Witched At Birth
2. What Not to Were
3. Witch Is the New Black
4. White Witchmas

Non-Series

Whose Bride Is She Anyway?
Polanski Brothers: Home of Eternal Rest
Sexy Lips 66

Accidentally Paranormal, a Paranormal Romantic Comedy series

Interview With an Accidental—a free introductory guide to the girls of the Accidentals!

1. The Accidental Werewolf
2. Accidentally Dead
3. The Accidental Human
4. Accidentally Demonic
5. Accidentally Catty
6. Accidentally Dead, Again
7. The Accidental Genie
8. The Accidental Werewolf 2: Something About Harry
9. The Accidental Dragon
10. Accidentally Aphrodite
11. Accidentally Ever After
12. Bearly Accidental
13. How Nina Got Her Fang Back
14. The Accidental Familiar
15. Then Came Wanda
16. The Accidental Mermaid
17. Marty's Horrible, Terrible Very Bad Day
18. The Accidental Unicorn
19. The Accidental Troll

The Plum Orchard, a Contemporary Romantic Comedy series

1. Talk This Way
2. Talk Dirty to Me
3. Something to Talk About
4. Talking After Midnight

The Ex-Trophy Wives, a Contemporary Romantic Comedy series

1. You Dropped a Blonde On Me
2. Burning Down the Spouse
3. Waltz This Way

Fangs of Anarchy, a Paranormal Urban Fantasy series

1. Forbidden Alpha
2. Outlaw Alpha

Made in the USA
Coppell, TX
29 January 2021